ANTiCiPATED RESULTS

Other books by Dennis E. Bolen:

Stupid Crimes
Stand in Hell
Krekshuns
Gastank & Other Stories
Toy Gun
Kaspoit!

ANTICIPATED RESULTS

DENNIS E. BOLEN

Arsenal Pulp Press | Vancouver

ANTICIPATED RESULTS
© 2011 by Dennis E. Bolen

All rights reserved. No part of this book may be reproduced or used in any form by any means—graphic, electronic, or mechanical—without the prior written permission of the publisher, except by a reviewer, who may use brief excerpts in a review, or in the case of photocopying in Canada, a licence from Access Copyright.

ARSENAL PULP PRESS
#101-211 East Georgia St.
Vancouver, BC
Canada V6A 1Z6
arsenalpulp.com · dennisbolen.com

Photograph of the author by Patrik Jandak
Book design by Shyla Seller
"Kitty" appeared in *The Arabesques Review*, October 2006
"I Drove" appeared in *The Scrivener*, McGill University, December 2006
"Fractionating" appeared in *Front & Centre*, Autumn 2007
"Anger" is anthologized in *Body Breakdowns: Tales of Illness and Recovery*, Anvil Press, 2007

This is a work of fiction. Any resemblance of characters to persons either living or deceased is purely coincidental.

Printed and bound in Canada on 100% PCW recycled paper

Library and Archives Canada Cataloguing in Publication

Bolen, Dennis E. (Dennis Edward), 1953-
    Anticipated results / Dennis E. Bolen.

Issued also in an electronic format.
ISBN 978-1-55152-400-9

    I. Title.

PS8553.O4755A78 2011   C813'.54   C2011-900764-9

In Memory of Bruce Serafin

"This is how things are."

Contents

PART ONE: PROBLEM
- 11   Paul's Car
- 23   Bip, Bip, Bip …
- 41   I Drove
- 50   The Pathetics
- 55   A.A./N.A.
- 64   Detox

PART TWO: PROCESS
- 75   Fractionating
- 89   Wood Mountain
- 104   Circumspection Man
- 115   Kitty
- 127   Clean or Dirty?

PART THREE: OUTCOME
- 139   Rocks, Ice, and Snow
- 161   One of the Winters
- 173   Anticipated Results
- 188   Qualicum Beach
- 203   Anger
- 211   Liza's Gig
- 214   Arch Sots and Tosspots

Part One

✗

Problem

PAUL'S CAR

In his sleep he thought to call out.

When he woke up, as Paul tells it, he still had to fight for comprehension. When you drive 100,000 kilometres a year over the same terrain and in your working life you have worn a dozen hardy vehicles into scrap and you have heard about other people being hit, but never yourself, and don't take notice of vehicular accidents when they are featured in sanguinous detail on the TV news, it takes time to understand that you yourself have been halted, battered, and nearly slain, deprived of routine and separated from comfort—T-boned actually, and flung into a water-filled ditch—by a truck running a stop sign.

A mystery truck, it turned out. Damage to its front end did not disable it enough to prevent the driver—Paul never knew if it was a man or woman—fleeing the scene.

He leaves for the cab-stand every 4:15 a.m., Paul does.

Drives the Honda to pick up a sublet mid-nineties Caprice Classic with 400,000-plus klicks. His wheel manner on the flat empty roads is automaton, near-doze, eighteen-year taxi-professional.

Touch the computer screen. The log-in routine.

On this day, around 4:45, Paul's readout paid him a trip from somewhere out in the woods.

Hints of sunrise etched the open areas. He sped along alone, liking the open pavement before him and secret dark of low scrub. In the absence of traffic he kept the cab mid-road, away from the watercourses on either hand.

A pickup truck with no lights materialized from the trees to his right. He watched sidelong, noting its progress over the culvert, past the stop sign, expanding in size as it came on toward him across the gravelled apron.

Paul was reluctant to accept that something was about to happen, given the cab/truck/speed/intersection vector. After too long he could only think about moving his brake foot. But brain and thought and movement were a slush of conflicts in this moment of inaction. At point of impact he was astounded at the persistence of his disbelief—denying visible evidence—even as he launched from the seat sideways, the open side of the shoulder belt letting him fly.

The city is an exploding suburb on a Fraser River delta named Lulu—after a San Francisco dance-hall performer—a vast murk of silt, deep channels of mosquito-rich water, condominium developments, shopping malls, airport, and vast groves of thick alder forest. Relevancies to Paul on an average day would have to do with where in the week it was (Friday), the season (spring), religious holiday if any (when the Sikh or Hindu drivers might be at temple), whether or not the cruise ships were in (meaning a possible 300-dollar day and tips in US funds), the cost of fuel, how efficient was the dispatcher. Et cetera.

But now within the shock-charge of danger, time was static, lacking value and length. He couldn't remember anything and he forgot nothing; driving, losing track, waiting out the transition between recall and oblivion. His mind was full of something—he couldn't tell what—and empty. He stifled a mental chuckle, flying cross-cab alone, at just how much he had of nothing. Nothing was his primary possession. Even the steering wheel lately in his hands was borrowed. The seatbelt now loose enough to let him leave was not of his possession. His life might be accounted for by phantoms, trading in ellipses, haggling over conceptions. Otherwise and essentially, Paul's life to him now was just a lot of impalpable motoring.

He was alone when he came to, the cab capsized driver-side in ditchwater. He hung hooked, part-way through the passenger window; arm and shoulder paining him awake, glass in hair, lower body hanging across the length of the front seat. Shoeless feet grappling at the steering wheel.

Paul tried to ignore the granular glass chewing at his armpit and shifted, but barely, because of pain. He noticed a bothersome clamour about him in the air; whining, slamming, cracking, and grunting. He stopped, disgusted to hear himself struggle so. Weirdly, save for his gasping and despite the discomfort, he could appreciate the calm of the morning. After a moment he could discern the slow ticking of the cab's dead motor and a malevolent rumble from somewhere mysteriously below.

Silence.

Then the rumble again.

The car, he divined, was slipping downward. Several minutes passed, by his reckoning, before Paul mentally received the significance of this.

And worse, as he struggled with one good hand to find relief from the aches grinding at him, he did finally disengage from the jagged window and slump coiled into the wet side of the car.

The cold jolted him. His clothes went chill so rapidly his heart stopped for an instant. He marvelled that he could keep breathing. The side windows were gone. In the gloom he could sense water flow around the upholstery. Noticeable current. Level rising. He turned himself around so that his face was out of the water. Pain became like a separate character, nearly addressable; the shoulder panged its own special torture. There was blood on his good arm where it had brushed his head.

Paul wondered how long this might go on before he screamed. He spat a mouthful of mouldy water, tried to raise himself by way of a one-armed chin-up on the gear shift. He fell back down. The car shifted again, a deeper stream of ditch water sluiced him. A shiver seized him from anus to scalp and nearly blacked his vision. He came to understand that he might not have much more consciousness in which to arrange survival.

Then through the deadly ditch quiet the first bars of "In-A-Gadda-Da-Vida" sang to him from wherever his cell phone had settled. Paul manoeuvred head and arm around, ignoring agony, and could discern it nowhere. He generally kept it in his inside jacket pocket, but it wasn't there now. If it were, he reasoned, it would not be ringing because it would have been water-shorted.

But it warbled on, regular and blasé. *"Doncha know that I love you ..."* To shuddering Paul, *Iron Butterfly* now represented a confounding normalcy, oddly insulting under the circumstances. *"Doncha know that I'll always be true ..."* But then this strangeness of mood passed and the chime brought him clarity. *"Oh woncha come with me, and take my hand?"* He belched a laugh-cry and coughed at the pain deep in his chest. This grave tune—*"And walk this land ..."*—he understood, and the simple act of answering it, might well contain his life.

The phone sang and sang. He could not see it. The song stopped.

Exhausted to the marrow, he settled back down. His gaze tracked up toward the subtle morning light-rise, taunting sweetly through the grey hole of the passenger window. The car settled again and the dash lights flickered and dulled.

Paul saw then where the cell phone was.

A green glow blinked at him from the hand-well of the passenger door, just below the latch. The missed-call flasher. Paul gazed with welling eyes. He raised his good arm, then let it fall back down, sapped and paralyzed, despairing, ready to swear and sob, straining for an impossible levitation. Cold, he realized, was near killing him. His injuries alone immobilized him. The phone might as well have been on the other side of town.

Whether or not the phone was his actual salvation is one of those speculative questions we would debate over drinks years into the future. Later that day at the bar Paul confessed that he simply cried, wept effusively for a long time.

"It wasn't just my buggered-up arm and hypothermic body that I was grieving about. I was cursing at the down-time it was going to cost …"

"Somewhat presumptuous of you at that point, no? To assume you'd have time of any kind. Down or otherwise." Bill diluted his pessimism by taking a drink in mid-interruption. "But okay. What happened next?"

"I tried a couple of more times to get the phone."

"You mean you didn't?"

"Hell no. I was bogged in that water with seatbelts tangled in my legs. Freezing. Shoulder hanging off me like a chunk of butchered meat. I couldn't get near it."

"So stop killing us with suspense. What finally happened?"

"I passed out." Paul smiled slightly, enjoying—I strongly suspected—the sight of eyes upon him around the table, hands upon pints, breaths held. "Then some guys came along and pulled me out."

"Wow."

"Yup."

"They just happened by and saved your skin?"

"That's what happened."

"Who were these guys?"

"Don't know. Cops say they didn't leave their names."

"And this all happened this morning?"

"Yup."

"That's why you're here, like …" Bill checked his watch. "About an hour early?"

Paul flicked his wrist. "Damn. My Bulova is gone."

We all sat a minute.

Gus signalled for the server to bring us more. "When does all this bandage-work come off?"

"Damned if I know. They were so busy in there I got up on my own and buggered off."

"You just left? Without saying goodbye?"

"Why not?"

"You didn't get an official discharge from the hospital?"

"I'm gone. They must know that."

"Wow, man."

"So what's the problem?"

"Paperwork. They hate that kind of stuff."

"Prob'ly looking all over for you."

"Well I was fine. My clothes were dry and hanging off the back of a chair. Wasn't going to stick around."

Paul's Car

"Did they pump you fulla dope?"

"They gave me something but it didn't do much good." Paul gulped at his drink. "It still hurts all over."

"So anyway, and by the by ..." I smiled at Paul as much as I could, but the bandage at his temple fretted me. "You probably shouldn't be drinking."

"You probably shouldn't be handing out unsolicited advice."

"Just sayin'."

"I'm okay."

"If you say so." I took a drink. "How was business before all this happened?"

"Considering the fact I didn't even get my first fare of the day, crappy."

"Well ... nevertheless. I don't know about you, but I think this goes to show what I've always said about your work."

Paul grimaced. "Which was what again?"

"In view of its demonstrated association with sudden death, that driving cab is not irrelevant."

Bill plunked his empty glass on the table. "Is that s'posed to be funny?"

The server put a new one in front of Paul, who smiled up at her. "Driving cab in and of itself is one of life's most deadening fates, an admission of non-life. Serious as all hell if you think about it." He frowned at me. "But a life-threatening car accident is the most banal thing in the world. The two together equal nothing. The two together have no relationship in view of the fact that one is slow and one is quick, a person chooses one and blunders into the other." He took a drink. "Thus, this stuff this morning is just action without meaning, lacking any kind of useful relevance."

"Paul, you get relevance by virtue of the story structure you have to offer. Listen to me. The banal beginning. The banal ending here in the bar. The unconscious middle is the fascinating part because it's what can't be verified. You let the first and last determine the centre. You write it all out, whatever it is, boring or exciting. Like a story of a janitor in a building; all the mops, brooms, wipes, cleaning products, endless nights looking out the windows of deserted buildings into the empty dark night, stuff like that. When you get to the end of it, all it turns out to mean was … I dunno. Perfect marble floors or something."

Paul smirked. "Little khaki badges on your shirt with another guy's name on it."

Bill snorted. "A steam engine when the guy was a little kid."

"That's the idea, boys." I was buoyed but not particularly optimistic; they were a hard crowd. "We can't listen to a story like Paul's without paying the debt to happenstance. To the vacancy between relevance and irrelevance. To the emptiness of question and answer. Content is misleading and deceptive. Not to mention the elegant literary device at play here."

"Device?"

"Yeah."

"Like what, repetition?"

"Exaggeration?"

"Illiteration?"

"No, I think you're thinking of alliteration. 'Illiteration' is something like what you are, Gus."

"So what already?"

"Elision. The act of leaving out. You suggest the first and last, and the middle fills itself in. Brilliant. The stuff of good literature. I've always said you should write, Paul. Haven't I?"

"All the time." Paul grimaced.

"So you see. When you look at this from a distance I believe you see permanence. The kind that stands alone and declares itself. Despite the irrelevance and insignificance and reputed banality of its content."

"I'm alive. That's important."

"Who were those guys? That's important too."

"Which guys?"

"The guys who pulled you out."

"This is all crap." Bill was miffed nearly for real. "Literature requires intrinsic value. You're talking about hearsay, Paul's perspective alone. It's too perishable. You can't make a silk novel out of a sow's newspaper item."

"I'd debate you on that."

"It's a useless thing to talk about."

"Oh, come on." I turned to Paul. "I bet there's a thousand stories you could tell about the cab stand."

"Only one." Paul winced and pulled at his sling. "I have to be there every morning no later than five a.m."

"That's a good start."

"That's an early start."

"You could write about how the morning chill dampens but does not extinguish your desire to be the best driver on Lulu Island at any given time."

Paul was listening but had lost interest. "Or you can just drink your drink." He looked at the table; we were all around. I sensed no desire in the others to further this discussion. But discussion was about all this crowd had ...

Bill says it all started one afternoon when Paul showed up with a bottle of up-market gin under his arm. Paul counters that it was Bill's roommates Gus and Nick and some other guys who came over that got things started in dead earnest. They'd first formed a talk crowd halfway through community college. English Lit.

Whatever the truth, after non-stop six-packs, cases, boxes, jugs, magnums, kegs—many fuzzy days and specious rationalizations later—the group of them decided this was the way to go and pledged to suspend work for as long as possible and sell off their assets one by one to invest in drinks.

The year was 1976.

Paul recalls vehicle registration and transfer documents lying around the kitchen. One bright Sunday he awoke and, after a thorough riffling of the fridge and the bedroom closets and the back porch, stared out a window into the brutal morning and thought it prudent to declare: "We're out of booze."

From the living room floor Gus called: "Is my van still there?"

Paul rubbed his eyes. "The yellow one?"

"'67 VW."

"Yeah, it's there."

"We'll drink it."

"Yo."

At times there was intelligent discourse. Members of the coterie drifted in and others wafted away. For a time, they'd get dressed up and go to discos in search of women. Over the years they'd had some soaring involvements—parties' full—and the inevitable cohabitations. They shared some of the girlfriends. A few had hung around long enough to nearly become one of the guys. Eventually the women were all put off; petrified food-scars on the walls, dents of flying crockery.

Paul's Car

From what Paul and Bill, Gus and Nick, and later on a-guy-who-used-to-come-to-the-bar-but-I-never-learned-his-name can remember, every few weeks they'd soberize and confer on what next to liquidate.

All the cars went. This took time because, in those days, guys would often keep more than one, sometimes several. Paul says he owned a nice '58 Pontiac and a '60 Chevy half-ton. But his pet was a '65 Rover 2000, loaded with whiz-bang gadgets. Paul and Bill were relatively well-off, having worked summers in the Alberta oil patch and down in Texas.

They got good money for Bill's near-new Monte Carlo. After a while, they started clearing out boats, trailers, motorcycles, ride-'em lawnmowers, mini-bikes, go-carts, ten-speeds—any kind of toy they had around.

The cars-for-drinks phase lasted the better part of three years. After that they trickled back to work but old habits die just about never, especially where booze is concerned. Bottles in glove-boxes. After-work beers stretching 'til dawn. The bar became their Community Centre. There was guy-strife, marital discord, liver damage, mental breakdowns, DWIs. Through attrition the whole thing officially broke up after a decade.

Paul stayed at it though, full-on, going it near alone. Being that he ended up solitary, still driving cab, on-the-bottle daily, it was no surprise. He's the classic rut-runner, a totally addictive personality and damn near powerless over it. He's the first, last, and everyplace-else-in-line to admit it. A year ago he tried to quit cigarettes. Got the pills, patch, laser therapy, counselling, gum, sold all his ashtrays, everything. He lasted three days.

Bill and Paul are the final bar regulars around which the stragglers, late-comers, fringe types, and grunge tourists gravitate. Since they banned smoking, Paul has to get up every ten minutes and go outside.

He shifted uncomfortably in his heavy bandage and showed me where the glass had bit into his armpit.

"Man, that looks like it smarts."

"Sure does."

I noted a grease patch on his hand. "The accident?" "Naw. I was working on my car. Oh yeah. You got a tool kit on that bicycle of yours?"

"Yeah."

"I've got to adjust my idle."

We went to the parking lot and got my tools out of the pannier. Paul started the Honda and yanked up the hood. We tinkered and listened.

The hum of the motor was monotonous. Eventually Paul went to shut the thing off. He lurched, reaching in to get the key.

When the motor was quiet, I said: "It might be okay now."

Paul tossed the door shut. "Yeah." He pulled smokes from his jacket.

"So, seriously. How's work?"

"Just awful."

"Hoo ... man."

We stood for a time in the sunlight.

"What are you reading these days?"

Paul exhaled smoke. "Oh, lots of stuff." He wielded his good arm to slam down the hood.

BIP, BIP, BIP …

Rightly or wrongly it was me who suggested we throw a dinner party, though because Paul can't smoke anywhere else I assumed it would be at his place. But somehow it evolved that because it's bigger we would have it at mine.

So I borrowed Simon's harvest-size table he got from IKEA. As he and his girlfriend Joan were on the guest list, this was easy to do. Then it was me who went ahead and designed the menu and invited the guests and just assumed Paul would cook. He is such a damn good cook.

"I'm not that good. I didn't even get past intermediate pastry."

"Forget pastry. Your meat loaf alone is worth committing a crime over …"

Paul had had many people to his apartment for dinner. He had trained at—*but not graduated from, alas*—*Le Cordon Bleu*, worked in a hotel kitchen in Denmark, and could make things like *Coquilles St Jacques* and *vichyssoise* and rack of lamb and duck *à l'orange,* all while puffing on a smoke and watching the hockey game. He would dissolve between the living room and kitchen. You hardly knew when he went and when he returned. He was conditioned to have all his ingredients ready to go—*mise en place*, as it was called—and to know how to season each dish to the acme of flavour. He cleaned the kitchen as he went, so it didn't even look like anybody was working in there. And all the while keeping the perfect music on. I was persuaded that with him at my side it wasn't too much of a stretch to transpose all this finery to a seven-member dinner party at my place.

Paul liked my apartment well enough. It had a fireplace just like his. I had a backdoor stoop where he could go out and suck back a cigarette.

Saturday morning I went out and spent a shocking amount of money on a deboned organic leg of lamb. I gathered all the vegetables I thought we needed. Fennel. Yams. Yellow potatoes. Things I don't usually get. I phoned Paul in his cab. There was the sound of traffic on his cell.

"Busy for a change?"

"Yeah. Fares everywhere. Money coming in."

"My man, you sound like you're at it."

"At last."

"I hope you're not too much at it."

"What are you trying to say?"

"I'm depending on you."

"Why shouldn't you depend on me?"

"Because in half an hour you'll be headed for the bar. Right?"

"So?"

"So. I need you in a different place."

"What do you mean? Where are you?"

"I'm where I should be. In my kitchen with sixty bucks' worth of lamb sitting on my cutting board."

"Oh, that's right."

"What do you mean, oh, that's right? You agreed to do a dinner party tonight."

"Yeah, yeah, yeah—"
"So I'm doing the preliminaries like you said."
"Good. Okay."
"So remind me what's in the marinade."
"Oil. Vinegar. Wine. Garlic. Salt. Pepper."
"Okay, I got all that."
"Did you roast up the garlic like I told you?"
"Last night."
"Good. Did you get the rosemary?"
"I had some from before."
"Make sure it's not too dry."
"I made sure."
"Lots of salt."
"Okay."
"Balsamic."
"Got it."
"Lemon pepper."
"Yup."
"Extra virgin."
"Got 'er."
"Fresh parsley."
"Just chopped it."
"Okay. So you mulch all that stuff together and paint it on the meat."
"Right."
"Then you put the whole thing in a plastic bag with some cut up pieces of fennel and put it in the refrigerator."
"Got it."
"When do you want to eat?"
"I don't know. What do you think?"

"I don't know. Who's all coming?"

"Simon and Joan."

"Okay."

"You. Me. Nick."

"Yeah. Who else?"

"Well, we kinda owe it to Jeannie."

Paul did not speak. I could hear the traffic more clearly on the line.

"I hope that's okay, Paul."

"That's fine. I can handle it."

"She's been darn nice to us."

"I agree."

"So what if she brings somebody."

"Who's she going to bring?"

"Damned if I know. Maybe nobody. Or some show-boy or other. Maybe even a girlfriend."

"Hokay …"

"Paul. You'll be fine."

"Hokay. This is your thing."

"I thought it was our thing. It was our thing when we first thought of it."

"When did we first think of it?"

"You know."

"I don't know. I'm kind of clouded up over here."

"Well uncloud. This has to be a cooperative effort."

"Whatever."

"I want you to be here."

"I'm going to be there."

"I need your help."

"You have the skills."

"I need solid cookery talent on hand. So I can be the good

conversationalist."

"Simon's a good talker."

"Yeah, Simon is good if he's on. But we need a mix."

"You have Joan and Jeannie. You've got a mix."

"Don't start waffling on me."

"I'm not waffling."

"When do I put this thing in the oven?"

"Don't forget to sear it first."

"Oh. You sear it?"

"In a big pot. With a little oil and as hot as you can get it. You need that brown to get the sugars."

"Okay, now I know I need you."

"I'll be there. What time?"

"I told everybody six-thirty."

I spent the rest of the day cleaning the place and chopping vegetables, putting off opening wine until the first guests arrived. I seared the lamb as instructed and put it in the oven on its bed of fennel. Joan walked over from Simon's place, alone. I took her coat and gave a quizzical look.

"Oh. Simon's going to be a few minutes."

"Huh? He's never late."

"Well. Today …" Joan's sweet countenance flagged into a comic frown. "Actually he wanted me to tell you. He can come but he might not be such an entertaining dinner guest."

"Let me opine, he accidentally went too far into a new load of weed."

"How did you know?"

"Twenty years of close friendship. I've seen him comatose. How bad is he this time?"

"It was way stronger than he thought."

"So he's ambulatory, I take it. But semi-catatonic."

"I think that's the word."

"Oh man. The only guy I know beside me who's got decent conversation skills and something to talk about and he gets slain by a viral batch of BC Bud. I hope Nick's on tonight."

"Everything will be fine. Paul is cooking for us …"

"Ah, well. That's another issue."

"Oh?"

"Never mind. Let's start drinking."

"*Absolument!*"

I tuned the CD changer to random.

We sipped Chardonnay.

Joan sniffed the air. "I love the smell of warm rosemary."

"It reminds me of walks in the woods. Even though I've hardly ever walked in any woods."

"It reminds me I grew up in Quebec."

"Yeah, it has that eastern settled smell of feasts long ago. A tradition of meat-roasting. Established middle-class white people in comfortable cottages cooking animals in late fall. Affluence. Power. Leadership."

"Houses with servants."

"Politics. The entrenched servitude of the masses."

"All of that."

"I'm glad you're here, Joan."

"Why? Expecting trouble?"

"Yes."

The doorbell went off just as my heavy word hit the floor. The effect was so artificially melodramatic Joan started giggling and was still at it when I got back up the stairs with Nick close behind, his super-cold bottle nearly anaesthetizing my hand before I could plop it standing up on the cutting board. "Wow, man. What did you do? Dip this thing in liquid oxygen?"

"I like my whites cold. Near frozen. Like the landscape of this great country."

"Hah ha ..." Joan was still in a laughy mode. "Do you always talk like that?"

"Joan, meet Nick. Nick, Joan. You guys have something in common. You're both trying to break into art galleries."

"I don't know about Joan, but in my case I'd do better with a crowbar and tungsten drills."

"Oh. Do you paint?"

"After a fashion, I'm told."

"I'm a sculptor. Mostly in metal these days."

"Well it sounds like you might already have the tools on hand. Shall we get tanked up?" I handed Nick a glass. "And go break into an art space together tonight?"

"Joan is waiting for Simon to show up." I eyed Nick. "Her boyfriend."

"Of course. All the best ones are taken."

"Ohh ..." Joan was suitably demure but nonetheless enthralled.

Paul wandered in at seven and planted himself on a kitchen stool. He handed me a warm bottle of white. "Put it in the freezer."

I poured him some of Nick's frigid *Blanc de Blanc*. I watched his hands. I did not like the look of his face.

Simon followed a few minutes later. He took one glance at Paul and made immediately for the living room. I put everything on automatic pilot and herded the others there myself.

"I want scintillation ..." I swept my glass hand grandiloquently. "Pure intellect tonight."

Joan was game. "I've done my reading."

"Excellent."

"And what all's for dinner besides lamb?"

"Well let's see. Roast potatoes. Candied Brussels sprouts …"

"Sounds fab and smells even better."

"Just don't overdo the yams." Paul stood up waggling his empty glass. "I assume it's where it's always at?"

"I've got one going in the door of the fridge."

"Don't let's forget the one in the freezer."

"You'll have to help me with that, Paul …"

While Paul was by himself in the kitchen I heard the back door open and there were voices. Before I could get there, Jeannie had introduced her date, a gaunt, frowning young guy.

"Oh, hi." She turned to me. "Thanks for having us, dahhhling. This is Damian."

"Hey, hello." I offered my hand.

Damian barely gripped and lightly shook. "What's that cooking?"

"Lamb."

"Have you got strong wine? Heavy stuff? Like Retsina?"

"No." I spoke while noticing that their hands were empty. There was no paper-wrapped silhouette on the cutting board. There did not appear to be a bottle in Jeannie's handbag.

"Well you should."

"Oh?"

"If you're going to cook something leaden like lamb …"

We all let that statement hang as Paul poured the rest of my Chardonnay into glasses for the two of them.

Jeannie sipped and her face darkened. "I hope you don't mind. Damian has to be home by midnight."

"Why should I mind?"

"How late are we eating?"

"Soon. Not late. I guess." I turned. "When do we eat, Paul?"

"Accidentally."

"What?"

"On purpose." He wandered back to the living room.

Jeannie rolled her eyes. "I see he's the usual Paul."

"Aw, come on, kid. Don't be like that …"

I looked again to Damian. He appeared fascinated by every item in the room. I noticed how extra thin he was. All-black clothing. Large, shiny, platform shoes.

"… And besides …" I turned back to Jeannie. "I see you are the usual Jeannie, Jeannie."

"What's that supposed to mean?"

I narrowed my eyes. "Why didn't you bring wine?"

"I'm broke. And other than this …" She tipped her glass toward my face. "I'm not drinking."

"Okay. No biggie. But just go easy on Paul."

"Am I being hard?"

"Tonight, for some crazy reason, almost everything seems to be hard."

"Oh, surely he's not still pining."

"Pining? Of course he's still pining. Pining's a light word for it."

"Oh for goodness sakes."

"You know him. You went out with him."

"For three months. Two years ago."

"Elephants and Paul."

"You don't think he's still interested?"

As Jeannie and I talked, Damian had wandered away. I sensed he wasn't heading for the living room.

Jeannie leaned close. "Damian's just out of rehab." She narrowed her eyes. "Be cool, okay?"

"Rehab? We just fed him some wine."

"It's okay as long as he doesn't have too much."

"What rehab program allows for limited drinking?"

"The problem wasn't alcohol, okay? Just relax. I've known him since high school."

Joan walked in with two empty glasses. "I thought I heard voices. How are you, Jeannie?"

"Joan. You look lovely."

I heard the bathroom door close heavily. While the women got reacquainted I pulled the cork on another bottle and charged out to the living room. There was no conversation. Paul was sitting limp, staring doe-eyed at the fire. Simon was reading a CD cover. As I refilled glasses the bathroom flung open and Damian's hard shoes tromped their way on the hardwood into the living room. He held out an empty glass and gave a kind of smirk. The women entered the scene. I filled Damian's glass. We all seated ourselves.

"So, Paul ..." Jeannie's acting voice offered her interpretation of reticence and the concomitant amount of courage necessary to overcome it. "How's life?"

The look Paul gave her said no sale. "Oh, blih-blah, blih-blah."

As in awkward situations down through history, chance played a part: As Paul blithered and stopped, the music took a mechanical pause and the room assumed crypt-like stillness.

"Hey cool!" Damian's interjection resonated within the absence of sound. "There's documented observation of nonsense diction among South American tribes. It's considered a sign of hostility."

I pounced. "Thank goodness somebody in here took the trouble to

Bip, Bip, Bip ...

study anthropology. It's a balm for dinner parties the world over, don't you think?"

Joan giggled. "Thank you, Margaret Mead."

"Bullshit." Jeannie was sour. "You made that up, Damian."

"Of course I did." He tipped his glass all the way back, guzzling. "None of your friends would have picked up on it, though, you dumb skank. The least you could do is play along."

"It sounded fine to me." I chuckled hard, hoping for the best.

"It really was quite amusing." Joan was right with me. I could have kissed her full on the mouth.

"Behave, Damian."

"Oh just shove it, Jeannie."

"Bip, bip, bip ..." Paul was rising from his chair.

"Good man." I got up too. "I need your crucial help in the kitchen."

I followed him closely all the way there. He went for his jacket. When he turned I saw for the first time the thickness of his eye-glaze. Dead drunk. He must have had more than usual at the bar. Without a word he made for the door and was gone.

I stood there. I listened. The music was back on. Radiohead. Perhaps there was the murmur of voices.

The roasting lamb sizzled in the oven and the air was loaded with the evergreen scent of the rosemary. I turned the heat on under the vegetables, then pulled the salad out of the refrigerator and whipped up a vinaigrette. For a few minutes I was happy and alone. Then Damian marched through on his way to the back door. "You got an ashtray?"

"Yesirree." I went for it and stepped to the outside where he had a butt already lit. I placed the ashtray in front of him on the railing. He regarded me with a warped smile.

Back inside, I was in the middle of getting the salad bowls and the salad and the dressing to the dining room when the phone rang. I hardly ever pick up. Absolutely never when the least bit busy. But as I returned to the kitchen Joan bustled in with it in her hand. "I thought I should get it because you're busy."

"Oh. Umm. Could you tell them to leave a voice message?"

"It's Paul."

"Oh."

I dropped salad forks and napkins and took the phone.

"You don't have to blame me." Paul spoke before I could say anything.

"Are you coming back?"

"It's not my fault."

"Who cares about fault. This lamb needs you."

"You've got it under control. Goodnight."

"Aw, Paul, jeez ..."

"You don't have to blame me."

"I'm not blaming you. I just wish you were here."

"I've got to go to bed."

"But Paul—"

"You're okay. You're always okay."

"How do I know when this thing is ready?"

"How long has it been in?"

"One and a half hours."

"You got that meat thermometer I gave you?"

"Yeah. Somewhere."

"Stick it in there. If it's at 180 degrees right in the middle, it's ready." I crouched at the oven door. "It looks about right—190."

"Is it browned okay?"

"It looks pretty browned, yeah."

"Take it out right away and let it stand while you're doing salad."

"Okay. We're right about to do that now."

"Have you got it out of the oven?"

"Yup."

"Now cut along the joint and see what colour you have inside."

"Along the joint?"

"Or anywhere you have enough meat to get in there an inch or two."

"Okay. It's pink."

"Pink but not red, right?"

"Nope. Not red really. I mean, pink for sure. A little red in some places maybe."

"Let it stand for ten minutes or so and then carve it up and serve."

"Why don't you come over? I'll tell Jeannie to cap it."

"Never mind."

"Aw c'mon."

"Nope."

I felt time pressure. The meat steamed on its platter. Paul hung up. Damian clomped back through and turned for the bathroom.

Joan came into the kitchen looking pained. "Things aren't going too well, are they?"

"Well I wish I had my culinary consultant on site but things will get better, I'm sure."

"Can I help?"

Nick popped into the kitchen with an empty glass. "Why is it more lively in here than out there?"

"Because you're not doing your job, lame-o. Get back in and entertain."

"I can't do a good job unless I know who's single. How about Jeannie?"

"She brought somebody."

"Oh come on. She can't be with that degenerate punk."

"Shhh. He's in the bathroom."

"Doing what, I wonder ...?"

Joan grabbed a stack of plates. "Should I put these on the table?"

"I have to warm them first. Here, you and Nick open these bottles of red and make sure there are enough claret glasses out there. Then you can both be bus-people. And you can call the others to table."

Halfway through salad, Damian emerged from the bathroom and sat down. Conversation at that point consisted of Jeannie's detailed appraisal of her pre-law courses and Joan's progress or lack thereof in becoming a self-supporting sculptor. Nick seemed to be trying to take Paul's place as the group's most profligate drinker. Simon picked at his lettuce as if there were bugs in it. Damian grunted at a few of the things Jeannie had to say, then set to his greens like a den animal.

I did not stay to see and hear the full gnashing show but stole to the kitchen to put fork and blade to the still-steaming leg of lamb. Desperation and steam-fouled spectacles warped my surgery and I made a minor mess of the slices—slipping at one point—partially tossing the accumulated juice off the platter and across the front of my trousers. Joan saved me by mashing the potatoes, dishing the veggies, and ferrying the whole presentation graciously to table.

From the kitchen I could hear Jeannie holding forth to her trapped audience: the munching face of Damian, the blasé visage of Simon.

Later, during coffee and liqueurs back around the fireplace, the conversational impetus completely sagged. At one point, Joan said: "How do you get such nice fire logs? The ones I get are so oily-smelling."

"Oh, it could be a function of your chimney draught ..."

For the umpteenth time, Damian flitted up like a startled bat and clattered out of the room. I noted the time—nearing ten—and knew that the early-to-bed lady downstairs would be on the phone to our landlord about the noise any minute. Then I noted that he had not proceeded out the back. Other noises suggested he might be prowling around the study or the bedroom. I leaned back in my chair and closed my eyes, wondering why my entertainment luck had so run out. During a hundred social occasions things had never crashed like this. I opened my eyes and looked around. Even now, with just a good quip from any one of them—and a few good-natured rejoinders—things could transform.

But no. I heard motion in the kitchen. Damian coming back from his patrol.

Then a muffled explosion.

"Goodness!" Joan started.

Jeannie laughed. "Probably Paul ramming his car into the building."

Anger flushed me. "For chrissake, give the guy a break." I bolted back to the kitchen.

Damian stood bemused by the cutting board, pouring himself a heaping glass of wine. "I think your fridge is upset, man."

I pulled the freezer door open and the remnant of Paul's bottle tossed a frigid slap of semi-solid wine down my shirt. The cold seized me. I stood transfixed for a moment, fighting to hold a sedate expression on my face, then slowly closed the freezer door. I found a tea towel and started dabbing myself.

Damian stood grinning, swirling his glass. "Weird scene, man."

"Huh?"

"Like. Everybody acts as if they never seen each other before."

"I wonder why that is."

"Worse than a psychiatric group home, man."

"Is it really?"

"From what I've seen, yeah. When their meds are not quite tuned."

"From what you've seen?"

"Yeah."

"Uh-huh. Look, Damian. I hope you don't think I'm being rude." I finished wiping off and tossed the towel in the sink. "Did you snoop around in my study earlier?"

"Sure."

"Did you take anything?"

"Just information, man."

"Really."

"I like to see what people have."

"Did you find anything of interest? Care to psychoanalyze me based on my colour scheme or my vinyl collection or the era of my furniture?" Damian just stood grinning. "Or are you some kind of advance man for a team of break-and-enter artists?"

"Hah. Good one."

"Well?"

"Naw." He drank, eyes darting. "All you got is books, anyway."

Jeannie appeared, coat draped over an arm. "Oh!"

"Heh-heh." I had not intended to laugh but the tone of it was just right.

"You're all wet."

"That's a matter of opinion."

"Hah ha."

"It's nothing. Just a little home cryo-treatment is all."

Her face told me she would continue to ignore my attempted humour no matter how hard I tried. "I hope you don't mind, but we've got to go."

"Mind?" I fought an impulse to cackle insanely.

Joan and Simon appeared. "Thanks for everything."

"You're leaving?"

"Yes. It's late."

"Huh. It's late alright." I tried not to sound bitter but couldn't help it. "It's been late since early this evening."

Damian smirked.

Joan patted my arm. "I'm sorry about Paul. Is he alright, do you think?"

"Hah …" I hadn't meant to laugh, Joan was so in earnest. "Some time when we've got a couple of hours I'll tell you all about how not-right he is."

"Why bother?" Jeannie had her coat on. "C'mon, Damian."

I gratefully bye-byed and shook hands and kissed cheeks and waved from the door. Nick came stumbling down the stairs with his coat on.

"I hope you're not driving."

"Are you serious? I'm on the bus."

"Sorry for the awkward night."

"Hey. I got her number, man."

"Jeannie?"

"Of course. On one of the many extended absences of her devil-spawn date. What's the trip with that guy, anyway?"

"Who knows? Do you really want to?"

"Hell no."

"There you go. So good night. Ride the bus carefully."

"I will."

Nick tottered off.

Back in the kitchen the calm of the place was one of the most welcome things I can remember. It was the perfect occasion to have a quiet drink. All the bottles were empty, so I scraped some of the wine slush from the floor of the freezer. Enough to fill a clean goblet.

I pulled a stool from under the cutting board and sat down.

I thought of going to the CD player but then reminded myself of how lovely the silence was.

"Bip, bip, bip …"

I sipped my drink as it thawed—slowly—careful to let the glass splinters slip to the bottom.

I DROVE

We were supposed to leave at sunup but it got to be more like nine or ten before anybody was sober enough.

I drove.

It was six hours out of the sprawl, across the valley, through the Coast Range, and up the canyon to the Cariboo. Paul slept in the passenger seat and Elaine, one of Bill's wife's friends, sacked out on the back seat. The van was near empty—we were only going for three days—and most of the freight would be booze, which wouldn't be bought until we were almost there.

Doreen phoned to remind us to meet her and Bill at the pre-arranged gas-up spot. I was fading by the time we got there, nodding at the wheel, even with the noonday sun glaring down. Pulling off the highway and into the gas-bar felt like a lifesaving thing to do. I swiped a card through the pump and started filling.

Bill was across the island doing the same to his SUV. Back when he first bought it we'd had the obligatory eco-conversation I inflict on all oversized vehicle owners:

"It's ridiculous to drive such a monster when all you ever do is come six blocks from your house to this bar and back again."

"Mind your own business. I'll drive whatever I want."

"You know they call those things 'Exploders,' don't you?"

"It's an Explorer, smartass."

"Not if it's got Firestone tires. They're doing a recall or something. You'll just be driving along and the tires explode."

"Whatever. I think I got Michelins. So there."

"Just looking out for your automotive safety with an eye to saving the planet, Bill."

"Well shove it where the planet don't shine."

"Hardy har."

"You can be obnoxious, sometimes."

"But you keep me around as a gad-fly, right?"

"More like a garbage fly ..."

But today we just stood mute, filling our gas tanks amid the din of highway traffic. Given that we were supposed to be pals, the non-communication between us got uncomfortable to the point where I had to yield to an impulse to say something, anything.

"So ..." I had to shout over a slowing semi's screeching brakes. "Do we stop for lunch or anything?"

"Huh?"

"Lunch. I'm starved. And my eyes are going crossed from all the driving."

I'd never been on this trip. Bill's hobby ranch was one of the things everybody talked about. He was proud of it, proud he could afford it. When we were drinking, Bill would often touch my arm and say I should come up to the ranch with him sometime. I had always said I would love to.

I nodded toward the road. "They should have twinned this highway twenty years ago."

Bill finished gassing up without comment. I got back in the van and pulled us over to the mini-mart. Big hand-written signs in the windows promised a fast-food chicken-and-chips type of service inside.

I Drove

I nudged Paul. "Snack time."

"Huh?"

"I gotta go and use that can." I pointed to the men's room arrow on the wall. "And then I simply have to sit down and get something to eat."

"Oh, yeah." Paul looked around. "The chicken place."

"So it's a well-known established stop on the Bill journey to the farm?"

"We get take-out."

"Are you serious?"

"You're supposed to eat and drive." Paul rubbed his eyes. "Bill doesn't like to stop."

"No kidding. Bill doesn't even seem to like to talk. What's the matter with that guy today?"

"He goes down into an altered state. A kind of Zen. A happy zone of meditation, almost. To the point he seems to like the trip more than he likes getting there. You'll see. And there's a practical aspect to it; only way he can go six hours without a drink."

"Bill? Zen?"

"It's not so far out."

"Look, man ..." I took my sunglasses off for effect. "I kind of had a more relaxed image of this trip. I mean, one of the things I most like to do is sit in truck stop diners with pie and coffee, watching the scene. You guys ever do that?"

"Do what you like." Paul shrugged. "But we gotta meet them at the big grocery store."

I looked around. Bill and Doreen were pulling open the doors of the gas/tires/chicken place and lumbering inside. I had to urinate in an urgent way.

Behind us, Elaine yawned audibly. "You guys getting some chicken?"

"Guess so." I opened my door and stepped out.

So then, the other thing that got me about this trip was driving with chicken-greasy fingers. The grubbiness, even after you wiped vigorously, bugs me still; all that residual gunk, the stuff the gas station paper towels didn't clear. Viscosity under the fingernails ...

"Man." I chomped on a drumstick, one hand on the wheel. "I hate this."

"This is how things are." Paul nibbled on a breast. "No way to change it."

We met them at the supermarket and pitched in for a mountain of food, enough for a week. Then there was the booze. By the time we'd got everything the van was loaded full. There was the smallest pathway to the back seat.

"Now I see why Bill insisted we take two vehicles."

"No, you don't see." Paul was pulling the tab on a cold beer as we watched Bill and Doreen and Elaine standing by the Exploder, examining food receipts. "We took two vehicles because Bill can't stand to drive with Elaine in the car." Paul took a short slug off the beer. "That's why we took two vehicles."

"Politics, huh?"

"Family dynamics. It goes back a ways."

At the ranch we cooked up a huge dinner. By the time the steaks were done, everybody was drunk. Bill sat nodding quietly in a chair in the living room. Paul and I stood around the barbecue. The women were on the veranda, smoking, fingering the stems of their martini glasses. Nobody'd brought any music, so we had to listen to the radio.

Next morning, Paul cracked a beer at nine-thirty. Doreen and Elaine slipped brandy into their coffees. We made a huge breakfast of the leftover steak. Aside from me, nobody had finished their dinner. By the time everything was ready, Bill was off-limits. Doreen whispered to everybody that he didn't want to talk. That included sitting at table or even taking a plate on his lap. I had to throw a lot of delicious cheese-laden scrambled eggs into the trash.

I reluctantly accepted a beer about noon. It settled well, so I had several more. Paul sat on the veranda. The women wandered in and out of the house. At one point, Doreen almost started crying over the low tonic water supply.

That evening, Bill tottered out to the barbecue and remarked to Paul and me that given the perfect weather we were idiots not to have gone to the lake that day. "At least tomorrow we should ride some horses."

"I wouldn't mind." I toasted the idea with Chardonnay. "Who do we talk to?"

"I'll handle it." Bill poked at a piece of the salmon we were barbecuing and took a long pull of beer.

The next morning I slept late—until ten—hoping they would start breakfast without me. The smokers—three out of the five of us—were early risers. When I got down the stairs I said a cheery hello to Doreen. She swished past me.

Paul was in the kitchen, cutting up a baked potato from two nights before. "Don't talk to Doreen." He did not look up from his knife-work.

"I just tried to say hello."

"She's in one of her moods." Paul paused to sip from a liqueur glass. "Is there coffee left?"

Paul looked across the counter. "About a cup."

"Well there better be." I mock-raised my voice. "Or there'll be hell to pay!"

Paul didn't laugh.

Late in the afternoon we started hearing on the radio about an accident in the canyon. A motor home had crossed the centreline and smashed head-on into a semi-trailer. The highway was blocked in both directions. Two dead. It was the lead story on the news for the whole evening. We never did go horse riding.

That evening Paul and I cooked up a massive lasagna. Everybody raved about it. Bill had a small portion, picking at it with a fork. His mood seemed improved. At the back of the fridge we found a couple of bottles of cheap champagne. We drank them quickly and found more down in the basement.

Flutes in hand, Bill and I sat on the veranda contemplating the view. He gestured down the verdant valley with his nearly full glass. "This stuff is made just down the road." We gazed along the serpentine twistings of a major creek and could hear the periodic grinding of vehicles on a gravel road.

"Wine country, huh?"

Bill took a swig. "Such as it is."

We boozed determinedly because this was our last night. Paul killed the last of the scotch. After midnight I was swilling my final Pinot noir when Elaine came out to the veranda and lit up. She gave me a look.

The smoke lilted my way.

I moved to the front yard, climbed the picnic table, and considered the sky.

"What's out there?" Elaine spoke through her grey fumy veil.
"The air is clean."
"Oh."
"No big deal."

At five in the morning I woke up sickish, fearing nausea. For insurance I chugged a whole litre of water; filtered, not out of the tap. I got a few hours more sleep. The radio still talked about the big accident. There was no breakfast. We spent a couple of hours frenetically cleaning the house. I put myself in charge of the loads of garbage. Bill sat in the living room, quiet. As she cleaned, Doreen became angrier and angrier.

Paul and I packed our stuff and stowed it in the van. We left the empties in the garage for future redemption—the tradition, as Paul termed it, was "Bill's Maintenance Fund"—so our load was back down to minimal. The jobs in the house were all being done. While everybody else was inside I sat in the van and watched a sparrow play among the breeze-blustered trees at the back of the property. It flitted and stood upon wavering branches, then flitted again, a rust-coloured actor on a testy stage.

A hummingbird buzzed by.

I spotted a hawk patrolling the valley.

After a while, Paul came out of the house and got in.

Bill stepped off the veranda, car keys in hand. He did not look at us.

Paul snapped on his seatbelt. "Might as well get started."

"Where's Elaine?"

"Riding with Bill and Doreen."

"Oh? Diplomatic relations improved?"

"She says she gets a funny vibe off you."

"What?"

"That's what she said."

"That's ridiculous. Just because I can't stand the smell of cigarettes."

"Whatever. It's best to stay out of it."

"Amen."

"But it's going to cost you with Bill."

"Cost me what?"

"I don't know. But somehow someway it'll cost you."

"Huh." I stared off again into the trees. "Some trip."

"Whaddaya talking about? I've seen way worse."

"Remind me again why we came up here?"

"Haven't you had a good time?"

By the pace of things it looked like Doreen and Elaine had a good bit of packing yet to do. Bill struggled to fit all the stuff into the Exploder.

"Oh man. I don't know how to answer that question ..."

We left without saying goodbye.

After an hour my gut was roiling. "I have to have a banana or something."

"You're the driver."

We stopped and gassed up. I got an orange, cup of coffee and a couple of doughnuts. Paul dozed in his seat.

But he was awake for the drive through the canyon. We came around a corner and there were the highway department vehicles. A flag person slowed us right down. Yellow-vested workers swept black dust off the highway. There was a low-bed truck and mobile crane parked at the side. Pulling closer we could see remnants of wheels, tubing, scrap. A big hunk of melted plastic. What looked like various furniture frames. For a second you couldn't understand what it was. There was a massive burn mark in the road. Our tires rumbled when we drove over it.

"Whooeee." Paul craned around to watch the sight as long as he could.

"Yeah, man."

After a few minutes the phone started ringing. Paul answered but there was no conversation. "Damn." He stabbed the off button and gazed out at the close mountains. "Bad reception."

The phone rang again and then stopped for good.

Behind, somewhere, was Bill.

THE PATHETICS

A while after that I have to confess I availed a woman to Paul when I shouldn't have. It was somebody I had dated but didn't want to see anymore. I suppose there's an argument against sexual brokering at any time, but the poor guy hadn't had a significant girlfriend in three years.

She was a fine enough match as far as it went. As fine for Paul as she was bad for me. Tending toward pretty. Just the right age. Damned smart. She'd worked as a rocket scientist at one point, a systems engineer for a blue-sky contractor or something like that. Then tried architecture. When Paul and I knew her she was working on a degree in urban design. There were all kinds of little mini-mall prototypes around her apartment.

I'd been put off by the way she left a whirring computer going near her bed day and night. There was also her substance abuse—she drank and puffed ganja every spare second—but we didn't last long enough to get concerned about that.

When Paul noticed we weren't seeing each other anymore he asked for her number. I gave it, thinking not a moment into the future. A week later they were lovers and for the first time in years he started to smile and laugh without reason and actually leave his living room to see movies. They ate in restaurants and spent weekends out of town. Took little boat cruises. Whenever I was around there was constant cuddling. It was easy to forget she and I had dated. I found it reassuring to celebrate her as Paul's completely. He beamed widely and nearly quit cigarettes.

Paul's apartment turned into a couple's nest, a place not entirely welcoming to me. We'd watch the hockey game with her curled up on the couch like a tabby. It was okay that she left the room frequently and came back smelling of burned rope; she made him happy as hell.

He began to narrate their lives together, gleeful about how compatible she was with his friends and relatives. "She shared the driving and the cooking and we slept in the guestroom like human beings!" Paul told and retold me about a trip they'd taken to see some friends up country. "Sally and Phil like her."

I had no opinion about how fast things were going—this was only about three weeks in—but I semi-enjoyed the proceedings right along with him.

They went to Las Vegas and Paul drunkenly phoned late one night. "We keep hitting our heads on the walls!"

"What? You're so drunk you can't stand up straight?"

"No. Well yeah but … It's the walls, man. They're slant!"

"Oh. You must be staying at the Luxor. Is it shaped like a pyramid?"

"Yeah, that's it. You can't even look out the window without bashing yourself."

"Yeah, okay. Just watch yourself, alright?"

"We're having a great time."

"Just don't come back married, okay?"

"Huh?"

"You heard me …"

As fun as it was to watch giddy new love, I was relieved when they came back unmarried.

But the good times rolled on: They went to farm country and played on a hobby ranch. Considered buying a dog together. Got sweet over her getting a speeding ticket in his car.

They were so damn cute together it was hard to say anything, and harder still to see what might be happening. But at a certain point a line got crossed; all the magical togetherness becoming the source of a weird, growing sense of indeterminate discomfiture.

One Sunday, they had me over for brunch. I brought wine for me and champagne to share. They also had champagne. Then there were the Greyhounds. When the vodka was gone we watched football with beers. She disappeared and reappeared, as was her wont, with the smell of hemp-smoke normal as air freshener.

Late in the afternoon she and I spoke about her work:

"I don't understand the big fuss about the big robotic Canada arm." I fumbled for my glass. "Although I could use one about now."

Paul whipped out vinyl and put on *Weather Report*. "Now drink your drinks and listen. These guys were terminal."

"Fuss?" She spoke soberly.

"I mean, what is it if it's not just a straightened-out coat hanger with a computer hookup?"

Her eyes nearly crossed. "You are not that stupid."

"You've never heard of humour?" I burped. "You should try it sometime."

"When something's funny, I laugh."

"Then go ahead and laugh. You're stoned enough aren't ya? Cut 'er loose."

"You're just pathetic."

"Pathetic can be funny."

"Pathetic is sad. That's all it is."
"In my life I'd have crashed and burned long ago without humour."
"Do you talk to all your friends like this?"
"Like what?"
"Like you're the only person in the room."
"Of course not. Was I doing that?"
"Do you ever listen?"
"To who? Whom."
"To anybody. To yourself, even. Especially yourself …"
Paul slumped onto the couch. "What's with you guys?"
I excused myself and went home.

Paul and I did our usual mid-week phone check-in. He sounded down, like the old Paul.
"How's the cab business?"
"Haven't been driving."
"What?"
"Haven't been to work in two days."
"And today's the third. You can't afford that."
"I'm in love."
"In hock too. I hope I don't have to remind you."
"Whatever. I'm pretty hungover. Damn sick, as a matter of fact."
"For two whole days?"
"We kept going after you left."
"Where's she?"
"Home, I guess. Working on her thesis."
"Wasn't she hungover?"
"Some I guess. But nowhere as bad as me. She can sure drink."
"Yeah, she sure can …"

Normally Paul would have been supremely irked at any loss of income. Not this time. Apparently she'd got right up Monday morning, left Paul's supine body to its fate, and marched out to do her thing.

A little time went by and then one night Paul threw supper on during a hockey game and announced: "Well. We broke up."

"How so?"

"In a glass-bottomed boat."

"Go on."

"She ended it."

"You went for one of your little cruises?"

"We were going to spend the night at the hot springs." He sighed. "That got trashed."

"And so it's over." I took a drink, keeping my eyes on him. "Done and kaput?"

"We'll see what she says."

We watched the TV.

Paul intended to call her after a time. Meanwhile, there were the shadowed lines around his eyes and the more-than-usual rounded shoulders.

Weeks later, after much extra drinking, he blurted: "I don't know why she did it."

All I could wish for was that he'd never find out.

A.A./N.A.

Kenny was a friend of ours who always had use of some kind of vehicle and never let us down.

He once drove me home from another town through a downpour in the middle of the night with me braced face-up in the bed of his pickup because he already had a full cab and I had to get home. I just had to get home.

Because Kenny wasn't drinking in those days he was our most dependable designated driver. He was also the guy to help you move, pick you up at the airport, procure sold-out concert tickets and generally hang with and be cheerful.

And that wasn't all. He could do a tune-up. Discuss movies and books and politics. Gossip with good natured, even-handed fairness. Fire off rapid stand-up comedy lines non-stop. He was extravagant in his congratulations for fortunate men, especially when the fortune had to do with women. It seemed to reflect something in him, luck with women. Not that he wasn't. During the time I knew him he had several involvements with intoxicating, intelligent beauties. Overall, Ken was a terrific guy. There was no end to the general positives.

Still, we didn't kid ourselves.

We were at Paul's place watching the ballgame one summer afternoon when Kenny turned up. With him was Gisela; a childcare worker, poetess, and sometime girlfriend of just about everybody.

We all watched the game. Paul and I were drinking, as was Gisela after we offered her one.

Kenny started yakking on. "We've got each other where we want each other."

Neither Paul nor Gisela seemed ready to engage him, so I bit: "What're you talking about?"

"It's like the international arms race and why we're all still here. Mad."

"What? You mean Mothers Against Drunk Driving?"

"No, no. The thing I've been doing lately."

"The thing."

"You know."

"Oh. The thing I know but I'm not supposed to know."

"Yeah."

"Okay, lemme get this straight. You've been mucking around in a grow-op business?"

"Right."

"And you're referring to criminal associates in said business, your intention to leave said business, and the Mutually-Assured-Destruction element of the planned extrication of yourself from the grow house you've been living in."

"Got it."

"Well …"

Nothing further was said.

We watched the game a while longer but anyone could tell Kenny was restless.

"Hey." He turned to Gisela. "Gimme your car keys."

Without a word she gave them.

"I'll be back in ten minutes."

We talked about him when he was gone.

"I'm pretty sure he's doing crack." Gisela was resigned.

"Oh man. I wonder if you should have lent him your car."

"I know ..." She wrinkled her brow. "But he's always been such a good head. I can't resist helping him out."

"Yeah, but there's helping and there's helping. Enabling is another thing altogether."

"He's way beyond that kind of stuff." Paul scoffed aloud and reached for his drink. "It's detox for him, now or never."

"And where's his car, anyway?"

"He sold it." Gisela tossed this out as if it were a crime report.

"Oh, come off it." Paul had his eyes on the TV. "Kenny hasn't owned a car in months."

"He's always got one."

Paul took his gaze away from the screen long enough to give me the narrowed look he always gave when I was being naïve.

Then we talked about Alcoholics Anonymous and Narcotics Anonymous. Gisela had been to an A.A. meeting, but neither Paul nor I had. She once took an old boyfriend who had asked for help. Nobody knew where he was now.

We hung around waiting for Kenny. The ballgame ended and Paul put on a DVD. Kenny never showed up.

Nobody saw him again for three years.

But my favourite Kenny story is the one where he went down to Los Angeles for a Rolling Stones concert—circa mid-nineties—and ingratiated himself into some movie-people circles enough to get a studio pass, a weekend in somebody's gazebo, use of a Porsche, schmooze-time at a premiere, and several other favours he mentioned but I can't remember now. He did it by dropping a name. He'd met this writer, a local guy whose reputation didn't reach out of the Pacific Northwest for all any of us knew. But Kenny had gone to a launch party, got the guy to sign a book, and used it to promote himself as an agent or producer or something around Hollywood for half a week.

The wild thing is that the writer—whose name I used to know because I once talked to him in a bar but I can't for the life of me remember now—started getting calls. He ended up scoring a couple of option deals as a result of Kenny's grand illusionary freeloading L.A. holiday. Kenny loves to tell the story. I'm sure at least some of it is true.

We know that he lived for a considerable time in the grow house—nine or ten dozen pot plants budding below floors—but it was never clear what his function was, to tend the crop or just use the top part of the place to make things look legit. It was always edgy with the kind of people you had to deal with in those kinds of situations. But edgy was Kenny's medium and his taming of the general wildness for the comfort and safety of his friends was what, to me, made him immediate and entertaining and good.

He had an irrepressibly sunny attitude about it: "If you guys ever hear I got disappeared, have a party."

I never heard whether Gisela ever saw her car again. But the good thing was that after I left that day she and Paul got going and they were good and close for quite a few weeks. Rekindled an ember that had cooled but not quite guttered. This was a welcome interlude for Paul.

So time went on and then I did see Kenny. It was during the annual jazz festival, he was sitting outside a coffee shop in the old part of town listening to an open air concert up the street. His head was shaved. He was with a bunch of guys who looked rough but cheerful. My own weird reaction to the scene made me duck and walk away, a single anonymous thread in the wide carpet of people standing around listening to the fusion sounds blaring from speakers on the sidewalk. When I paused, up the crowded street, I was ashamed. I thought of running back and saying hello. But then Kenny and his crew strode through the throng not far away and I felt again that I would not be able to talk to him that day.

Later on I mentioned my Kenny sighting to Paul. We were watching the playoffs.

"Oh yeah, I forgot to tell you ..." Paul put down his drink. "A guy at the bar says he's in rehab."

"No kidding?"

"That's what I heard."

"I wonder why he shaved his head."

"Male pattern baldness. I'd do the same if it were me."

"Knowing Ken, he's doing it for a laugh the next time he sees us."

Paul looked at me sidelong and did not say anything.

"I wonder whatever happened to Gisela's car?"

Paul shrugged.

"Where the hell did he go that day he said he would be gone ten minutes?"

"I can imagine ..." Paul lit a cigarette. "But nobody knows for sure."

I went for my drink. "What's your favourite Kenny story?"

"You mean besides this one?" Paul did not take his eyes off the TV.

"What do you mean?"

"Well the guy's supposed to be a good friend of ours, borrows a car out of this very room ..." Paul gestured with his cigarette hand. "Disappears for several years. Turns up at the jazz festival looking like some cult wacko. I'd say that's a pretty good one." He smoked. "I'd sure like to hear the shadings that go with it."

"I'm sure Kenny'll some day tell it to us with all the details."

"If he doesn't turn up dead."

That stopped me. "You think his life is that dodgy?"

Paul picked up his glass and gave me another of his looks.

I sat back and tried to watch the game. But a memory came to me about Kenny's housewarming party years ago at the grow house that we were never supposed to know for sure was actually a grow house. It was a nice place in a quiet part of town. Everyone wondered how he could afford it. Kenny claimed he was making out fine as a props man for a theatre company. The job was perfect, he said. He beckoned me to come up to a room in the attic. I thought he was maybe going to show me a nude photo of his latest girlfriend, a sweet-looking thing who Kenny said worked in a bank but we all knew had to be a hooker, if she existed at all. The only clue to who she was could be found in one of Kenny's proudly displayed faux paintings in the living room—on a background much like black velvet.

When we got upstairs Kenny flipped back some blankets on a dishevelled bed and pulled out a big black ugly gun.

"Whoa—what the hell is that?"

"It's an imitation Bren."

"Imitation?"

"One of those knock-offs they make somewhere in Michigan. A guy I know got it mail-order."

"Knock-off or not, it looks damn dangerous."

"It's not." Kenny offered the thing for me to hold. "Yet."

It was as heavy as two cast iron frying pans and startlingly cold to the touch. "Is it really a phony?"

"Just a little." He tapped a finger near the breech mechanism. "This needs some real parts. Then it shoots."

I wondered at the time why Kenny had anointed me with the knowledge that he had a replica machine gun. All I could come up with was his odd degree of reverence when we spoke once about my having been a teenaged military reservist and a target-shooting prodigy with trophy and crossed-rifle badge to prove it.

Then I remembered that it was that evening I had recalled to him the night of my wild ride in the back of that truck he used to have. How illegal it all was with me spread-eagled, feet and hands holding to the edges of the wheel wells, trying not to slide around and hit my head. What fun I had gazing into the black night, watching the streaming rain, the flashing ethereality of car and highway and ambulance and police sirens screaming their unseen way about me.

"It's a dumb thing …" I had told him. "But I think of it all the time. It's one of my favourite things to remember."

"I know." Kenny awarded me a smile. "It takes guys like us to act like that."

It was then that he showed me the Bren gun.

Paul and I sat and watched hockey.

I was chewing over the gun incident. "Did Kenny ever show you his replica machine gun?"

Paul winced at me. "His what?"

"He once gave me a look at this prop machine gun. A Bren, I think it was. I assumed it was from the movie outfit he was working for."

"And it's called a what?"

"Bren. I looked it up. It stands for Brno-Enfield. Ken explained it all to me. It's supposed to be British but it's not. It comes from some guy's garage workshop back east. A nasty-looking handheld machine gun pistol-like thing with ugly black metal parts and no wood stock or anything. Looked like it was made from an old fireplace grate."

Paul looked at me strangely. "I never saw it." After that, Paul seemed reluctant to discuss Kenny or that fateful day when we had last all sat in front of this TV. I remembered too late that Paul tended to congeal at memories of the long-departed Gisela. Their few weeks together were a brief beam of light into his otherwise drab life. He quietly sneered at me the rest of the night.

Later on, I had a dream that I was sitting in an A.A. meeting. There were the expected kind of people. Some of them looked like Kenny then and now. There was much talking and frequent weighty silences. I listened. The stuff I listened to was interesting and dreadful. Many spoke; I heard it all. I sat on a folding chair and tried to comprehend each verbal bit and sweated at the effort. My head kept pushing toward the image of me face-to-the-heavens in the back of that truck. Such was the speed at which Kenny piloted us through the night, the rain scarcely touched me save for a light pelting at my feet. The droplets from the sky drew a solid web of constricting lines down my vision, as if I were in a straw prison. The hiss of tires on the pavement. The oncoming cars and trucks each their own separate roaring presence. The underpasses dinned weird interludes of discord. Supine inside this miasma I was seized with a stark aloneness. There was indeed fear, but I reminded myself that Kenny was at the wheel. Him knowing that after a night of drinking I needed to be where he was taking me. So I relaxed. The whole wobbling ride was like a giant rocking cradle.

I woke up confused. Every story and every silence from the A.A. meeting was present. I picked the stories apart and turned them over in my brain to see if there were marks or textures from which I might take meaning. Somewhere along the line I noticed that the silent parts were for thinking and that comfort takes different forms for everybody.

DETOX

I didn't like the look of things when Gus showed up. He wasn't committed. This was going to take commitment.

"Paul." Bill took charge right off. "We're here because we're concerned."

Paul had poured himself one and was sitting on the couch. The easy sense that good friends were over to watch a football game was nearly gone but still showed vaguely on his face. "Concerned about what?"

"You gotta stop." Nick stood over him looking grave. "We're taking you to detox."

Paul's look faded to blank.

"We're not going to shit-kick you or anything. Heh." I spoke up in as assuaging a manner as possible, not liking the excess heaviness descending. "It'll have to be your decision ultimately. But we can't sit around and watch you kill yourself anymore."

Paul sniffed and wiped his nose. "You guys want a drink?" His eyes hardened.

"No. We don't want a drink."

"You sure? Because I could swear you guys are just a bunch of burned-out alkies like myself."

"We're not. At least, not as bad as you."

"Really? Gee. How could I be so wrong?"

"Stop it, Paul."

"I mean …" He put down the drink and swept his arms wide. "I only drink as much as everybody else."

I stared at him. "I only drink when I'm around you."

"Jeez, you're right, you know." Nick was nodding his head. "I only ever get excessively pissed when Paul's around."

"Um …" I was still bruised by the vacuity of all concerned during my ill-fated dinner party, and particularly Nick's sodden conversational impotence. "That's not exactly true."

"Knock it off, you idiots." Bill turned and reddened at us. "That helps a hell of a lot."

Gus snorted. "This is crap." He looked at his watch. "Let's get him out of here and stick him in rehab and get it over with."

"Yeah!" Paul attempted to get his drink back but misjudged the effort necessary to straighten himself from the couch. "Get it. Over with." He struggled and gripped the glass. "So you can all go to the bar."

"No, Paul."

"And have a few quick ones to congratulate yourselves."

"Don't try to talk us out of it." Bill nodded to the rest of us. "We hashed it out amongst ourselves. It's for us as well as you. It's no secret we all get a load on just about every day but in your case it's way out of control. I mean the impaired driving alone. We have to do this or we'll be sorry. And we can't have you doing anything to yourself. We could never live with our ourselves if we didn't."

"So you guys are solid, eh?"

"Well. You could never say that. But we agree on this."

"All of you?"

Silence.

"Don't make it harder than it has to be, Paul."

"I guess you had to come along on this." Paul turned to me. "They needed a van."

"If you wanna know the honest truth I was the one who suggested it in the first place."

This created another silence. Bill sighed and found a chair to sit in. Nick shook his head and crossed his arms over his chest. Gus grunted.

"Well, okay." Paul performed a deliberate abs curl and put down his drink. "If this is my last one, I guess I'll make a point of going slow. Enjoy it."

"We want this to be voluntary."

"Hah!" Paul glared at Bill. "I'd rather you picked me up by my arms and legs and packed me off. With conviction. With commitment. With real balls. If you were real pals and real men you'd do that."

"We don't want to do that. We can do it, but we don't want to."

"The program demands that you go on your own." I tried to sound solid. "Voluntary. Having realized you need help. Accepting of the intervention and assistance of your friends. We just essentially provide you the transportation."

"You crazy bastard." Gus was acidic. "We're here to tell you we're not gonna let you do it to yourself!"

"We can't drink with you anymore." Bill, Nick, and I spoke at nearly the same time.

"Well ..." Paul looked at us, then at his glass. "You sound like you've got it all rehearsed out."

"Sorry if that's what it sounds like."

"I never heard bar guys talk in unison before. Like a comedy routine."

"Don't make things harder than they have to be."

"Hokay. You don't have to keep repeating yourself." He picked up his drink, took a swig, then solemnly put it down. "What's the procedure from here?"

"Get your jacket." Gus huffed.

"But first ..." I glanced around. "Make sure everything's off. You might be gone some time. And phone up the guys at work. Tell them you need a couple of weeks."

"If you don't mind ..." Paul lurched from the couch. "If you guys don't mind." He tottered for the door. "I'll settle my affairs on my own." He snatched his jacket from the hook in the entryway.

We filed out of the apartment. With the crowd of us standing in the hallway, Paul flipped off his lights and slammed the apartment door closed. He patted his pockets.

"You won't need keys where you're going." Gus spoke with unnecessary gruffness.

"I need to lock the goddamn door." Paul yanked a lighter and a pack of cigarettes out of the jacket. "And these too." He produced keys and locked the lock.

I was fighting qualms, being part of all this. Despite long conversations the four of us had had—plus intense soul-scouring and a long session of counsel from Simon the psychologist—I still felt lousy. I particularly disliked the custodial feel of it all as Paul finished locking the door. We were standing with ridiculously lugubrious expressions in a cordon around him. It must have been at least semi-comedic. Paul paused and grinned at us. Then, with startling agility, he deked between Nick and me and ran down the hall.

"Whoa ..." Bill and Gus were slow to respond, given their bulk. Nick and I darted around them and made behind Paul as he disappeared through the stairwell door.

"Come on, man! Hold up."

There were no further words. We scuttled down the stairs and got to the building entrance as the big front door swung shut. I hesitated. Despite years of friendship and utter faith in Paul's passivity, I still preferred to have at least three guys with me when I tried to take his car keys away. By the time Bill and Gus appeared and we all hit the sidewalk, Paul was out of sight.

"Where does he park his car?"

"No particular place." I looked up and down the curbs. "He gets whatever there is on the street."

"Does he have a residents-only permit?"

I looked at Bill. "What the hell does that have to do with anything?"

"Over there and around the corner is just for residents." Bill pointed to the signs. "But over here and down that block there are general two-hour parking sections. So he's more than likely ..."

"You guys go that way and I'll go this way."

"Oh, for chrissakes." Gus pointed. "There he is."

A white Honda speedily approached and then slowed at the intersection. I knew if we did not apprehend Paul now—while he was still obeying traffic laws—we would not do him any good this day at all. As if the others had been thinking the same thing, we stepped as a unit into the street and faced down the Civic.

Through the windshield I could see Paul regarding us without passion. He edged the car through the crosswalk and slowly toward us. Three metres out, he stopped. We stared at him. He stared at us. Slowly his forehead met the steering wheel and his shoulders went limp. I let myself sigh. Then gears gnashed and the Honda chirped backward. Paul's arm was on the headrest of the passenger seat, his other hand expertly wheeling the car in reverse, accelerating along the narrow channel between parked cars. I watched—fearing a crash—and was nearly disappointed when he twirled unscathed into the alley, braked and shifted, then sped back out and away.

"Holy crap." Bill stepped carefully back to the curb. "How pissed up is he, anyway?"

"Paul can do that in his sleep." I reached for the car keys in my jacket. "He could do it in a coma. Any good cab driver can."

Gus chuckled. "He's one rangatang sonovabitch."

"Headed for the bar." Nick gazed after the disappeared Honda. "More than likely."

I opened the van door. "Let's get over there." Although the plan as it had formed over the weeks had been contested and doubted and debated thoroughly, I now received no contradictions.

We hustled the eight blocks and got a parking space by the door. Paul's car was not present. Nor was he sitting in his usual spot in the bar or in any other area. The waitress hadn't seen him.

I struggled to formulate a viable plan B. "We better call the cops."

"What are you talking about?" Gus slumped into his chair. "He's just out driving."

"He's tanked."

"No." Bill sat down too. "We better report it. What if he kills somebody?"

"Then he goes to jail."

"And we don't want that or the other thing." I pulled a finger of change from my jeans. "I'll make the call."

"Put your money away, lame-o." Gus's face was ugly. "It's a 9-1-1 call."

"Oh yeah."

He whipped out his cell and stabbed the keys with his thumb, then handed it to me. I stepped away and stuffed a finger in my ear to cut the bar sounds.

By the time I got off the phone there were drinks on the table. I hadn't noticed anybody ordering.

"For crying out loud, you guys!" I nudged the nearest glass away. "We just tried to get our friend into detox. He's out there somewhere impaired driving. We called the cops on him ..."

"You called the cops on him." Gus's demeanour wasn't getting any lighter.

"Well we have to finish the job somehow. And here you guys are drinking."

Bill sniffed. "You do it your way."

Nick shrugged and gazed into the suds at the top of his beer.

Gus turned to a football game and said nothing further.

There was a sound right then. Even with the place filling up of a Sunday afternoon—sports commentary from the jumbo TV; music system pumping out some kind of dance-mix pablum; the general drinking crowd palaver—it was unmistakably recognizable as a clash of metal-on-metal. We tensed. Someone called from the entrance, "There's a car jam out here."

One glimpse and I knew what had happened. Paul had bunted at low speed into the only side of my van that hadn't already been dented.

"I thought it was a parking space." Paul was struggling out of the driver's seat.

I held myself calm, intent on counsel. "You know damn well it's the walkway."

Before Paul could fully emerge from the Honda, Gus wordlessly strode up and rammed an elbow into the side of his head, snapping his skull back against an edge of the car frame. Paul dropped directly downward.

Bill and I stood immobile.

Gripping the door and car frame for support, Gus lifted a boot and stomped Paul below the ribcage. He stepped back and faced us with satisfaction, as if singularly mastering a pesky chore which had thus far defeated us all. "That'll do him."

Paul contracted into a fetal pose on the ground, his face darkening to mauve. Gus strode back into the bar.

A woman thrust a cell phone at me. "Do you need to call 9-1-1?"

I took the phone absently in my hand then dropped to my knees to see Paul. His eyes bulged. His face got darker. There was little breathing if any. I was about to hand the phone to someone and try to remember my CPR training when two pairs of black-clad legs appeared in my peripheral vision. An officious voice declared: "Ambulance is ninety seconds out."

I stood up and sidestepped casually into the crowd. I found the lady and gave her phone back. Bill and I edged with care through the crowd and away from the cops.

Gus was no longer in the bar.

Nick saw me looking for him. "He went out the back."

"Nowhere near soon enough."

"Yeah. Sorry." Nick took a drink from one of several near-full glasses on the table. "Yesterday I was in here. Moment of weakness. Bad day at the data centre. Anyway we got talking about our plans about Paul …"

"It was supposed to be just you, me, and Bill."

"I know, I know."

"So you let it slip."

"I only mentioned it in passing. Right away he said it sounded like it would be fun."

"An intervention? Fun?"

"Some guys are weird, man."

I took a seat. My hand shook as I tried to lift a drink.

Next day at the hospital, Paul was sitting up and smiling. "I might look fine but don't tell me any jokes. It hurts like hell to laugh."

"Don't worry. I have no material."

"Sorry about the van."

"I don't mind having a friendship relationship with you. But now we have a car insurance relationship."

"I hope it's not going to ruin anything."

"Who knows?"

We sat for a time talking about the work he was missing and the wisdom of avoiding the police in all circumstances and the best auto body shop and how the bar would be buzzing about this for a long time.

Part Two

Process

FRACTIONATING

When I got to the office my rubber soles were squishy like warm Jell-O. I ignored the reek and leafed the phone book to find a car dealership.

Rodney paced in talking: "I don't know, man. There's still no resolution to my mind ..." Rod and I had worked together for years and were friends before that so I'd seen him obsess over marks at college and struggle with cocaine and mess up a first marriage and fail, like me, to get traction in a career—we'd been flailing away at a property management firm for longer than was decent—so I wasn't surprised it took him a second to notice I wasn't listening. "Why does it smell in here? It's like you've been walking around in gasoline or something."

"In fact, that is exactly why it smells in here. I have been walking around in gasoline. Clean, fresh, smelly, dangerous gasoline." I kept flipping pages. "It leaked out of my car."

"Whoa."

"I'll say."

"What happened?"

"Well it was like usual but different. I stop for gas and put the nozzle in and pull the lever and start fuelling. I'm standing there daydreaming. Then the guy in the booth shuts the pump off. I look down and I'm standing in gasoline."

"Whoa."

"Then there's this sizzling sound ..." I looked up from the phone book, deciding to get Rod's mind completely off his troubles and onto mine. "And the guy says, 'Know what that steak-cooking noise is?' 'No,' I say. 'Gas dripping onto your tailpipe,' he says."

"Whoa!"

"I'll say 'Whoa.' You can say 'Whoa' again."

"Explosion hazard."

"No kidding."

"Lucky you don't smoke."

"I never smoked. I hate smoking. You know that."

"Better get it fixed."

I lifted the phone book and let it plop loudly back down.

"Wouldn't a computer be faster?"

"You know I'm old-fashioned."

"You just go to the White Pages site. Simple."

"While we still got these big hunks of paper around I'm gonna use 'em."

"Huh."

"Yeah. Huh."

"Anyway ..." Rod parked himself in a chair. "I can't figure out how to do it, you know? It just won't make sense either way."

"We've been through this so many times."

"I know, I know."

I returned my attention to the phone book. "Do you know anything about fuel systems, Rod?"

"Naw ..." He stood up and started pacing again. "She's no good in the sack. That's the real problem."

I found a number and reached for the phone.

"Well, I shouldn't say she's no good ..."

I held the phone to my ear, poised a finger over the keypad and looked at him. "But it's a sex problem in essence?"

"In essence, yes."

"And it's not specifically a technique or attitude or inner moral conflict problem as such?"

"Not as such, no. It's tough to figure exactly. I mean, I'm not a sex fiend or anything." Rod paused. "You know I appreciate your taking the time to help refine my issues here."

"No problem."

"Especially when you're ... you know. Trying to keep your car from exploding."

"I can't find the dealership that sold me the thing. They seem to have gone out of business or something."

"I'm hung up on this."

"Don't blame you."

"It's a mental kick in the crotch. So close to the date."

"You're for sure gonna have to work it out. It's crazy to just go along like there's nothing wrong when you don't feel comfortable with the whole thing. I mean, there's examples all over the place."

Rodney went silent, looking at me and knowing what I was talking about.

"And now look what's happened to my car."

"It must be a royal damn pain to have something like that go on you."

"It sure is."

"Absolutely."

"Stupid thing."

"It's still new, isn't it?"

"Five years old. And it was used when I bought it. But I just need a new filler hose or a grommet of a particular kind or attachment or some such mechanical thing like that." I mimed with the phone a nebulous auto part in the air above my head. "Probably put it in myself if I wasn't so hectic."

"Part'll most likely cost way less than the labour."

"I figure."

"Can you get any gas in at all?"

"Some, but not much. I'd have to sneak a little in every day and make a flammable mess everywhere I went. That'd get pretty thin pretty fast. A real nuisance. I'd be an outlaw to every gas bar person in the world."

"Yeah ..." Rod turned to the windows and gazed. "She doesn't even cook, you know that?"

"You're gonna have to eat out or end it, man."

Rod didn't laugh.

When I got the dealership service guy on the phone he sounded all serious and said they would check out the problem right away. I drove down there, walked into the office and spoke to the first guy I could find. "I got the gas tank problem."

"Oh ..." A man who looked like he was in charge overheard and came over. "You're the guy with the gas leak." He glanced past my shoulder to the service bays. "You didn't bring it in here, did ya?"

"No, it's out at the curb. You want to come look at it?"

"Naw." The man wrote on a form. "Just leave us the key."

"But you better see where it's leaking. I mean, it's kind of tricky. You might not find it; it only does it when you're filling gas."

"We'll find it."

"Are you sure? The problem seems to be in the hose between where you put the nozzle in and the actual tank."

"That's okay. We'll find it."

He took my key.

By afternoon I needed the car. Over the phone the man said it was ready.

"Did you find the leak?"

"Well they tightened up the clamps in there. They were kinda loose."

"But did you actually see where the leak was? How do you know it was clamps?"

"The boys were pretty sure."

"They were, huh?"

"And you just don't get that kinda thing with that type of car."

"You don't, eh?"

"Nope."

"With that type of car."

"Not that kind of thing, no."

"An inexplicable gas leak from somewhere around the filler hose."

"Yeah. We never seen one."

I grabbed a taxi down to the shop. The man handed the keys right over.

"You're sure it's fixed."

"Oh yeah."

I paid the price they charged and dashed away.

Next day at the office, Rod kept it up: "What do you think? A late-night flight to Rio de Janeiro under an assumed name?"

"Small-time jerkoffery." I shook my head. "You don't want that. If you're not going to take executive action and call it off, legit to everybody's face, then go through with it and quit your whining."

"Yeah I guess. The invitations are printed."

"And you've known her long enough. You should have some idea if you like her or not."

"Like her?" The notion seemed to hit Rod as fresh. "Hmm ..."

"If you don't like her now, based on all you know of her and all you think she's likely to become, then logic tells us there's no substantive reason you'll just magically like her later."

"I like her."

"Gee, that's great."

"I do."

"You do. Okay, you do."

"You can't stand her, can you? You told me that once."

"I don't actively dislike her. She's cute and everything but kind of a cow about it. Certainly more than she should be, commensurate with the actual grade of her cuteness. Or something like that. By my calculations, anyway."

"You're my friend." Rod was not looking at me. "I asked your opinion, so you're allowed to talk like that."

"I certainly wouldn't marry her."

"You don't have to. You just have to help me decide whether I should."

"You know what I mean."

"I don't know why I'm asking you. You're not exactly an authority."

"No reason to be sarcastic."

"Well you're not."

"You're my friend, so you're allowed to talk like that."

"Sorry. But you're just not a guy to testify about marriage, that's all."

"Some might say I was. Who do you know who's done more research? Anyway, whatever. I'd never tell anybody what to do or what not to do."

"Yeah, I guess that's a good policy." He turned back to me. "I value your opinion."

"Thanks. It's free."

"How are you doing with Sally?"

"Who?"

"You heard me."

"What do I need with her? After my history."

"Don't let it get you down."

"Never mind Sally. She's a fine person. I'm sure she can get along."

Rod smiled and sneered. "Whatever."

"I don't think I like your tone."

"Oh, relax."

"If you say so."

"Everything's cool."

"If you say so."

"I do."

We'd had this conversation before.

"Ask her out."

"Maybe."

"Have a good time." Rod was leaving as he said this.

Car-wise, though, I was having a hell of a time. I went to fill up and knew right away by the smell and the splash on the pavement. The attendant shot open his sliding glass window and leaned out. "What the heck you doin'?"

"Trying to fill up." I pulled the nozzle out.

The man glared.

"I've got a leak, okay? No big deal. Just don't smoke for a while."

"I'm gonna have to ask you to get that vehicle out of here."

As I drove away he got busy with a water hose.

Next day I was at the dealership sharp at eight a.m., trying to do a convincing mad-dog routine. I went away thinking it might have worked or it might not.

Later on I went back to pick up the car. Rodney gave me a lift. His driving was brisk and confident.

"You're sure having a lot of trouble with that thing. Time to trade it in."

"Hey it's the first time anything's gone wrong. Besides, I couldn't afford to buy the wheels off a new car right now."

"Oh." Rod's driving became conservative while he was thinking. "Yeah." He slowed the car right down. "I wonder if she'll ever do that to me."

"Well all autos get finicky. No getting around it."

"No, no. I mean her. I wonder if she'll ever nail me to the wall."

"Sooner or later maybe."

"Yeah."

"But cars'll do the same."

"What are you talking about?"

"I have an instinct about it. It might translate to some kind of personal philosophy. Something like: Don't spend your last dime on a car. Ultimately, it won't get you where you want to go."

"What else is new?"

"Nothing is new."

"Man, that's so empty."

"Like my gas tank. Last time I saw."

At the garage the man assured me they'd found the problem. "It was a buggered filler hose."

"A buggered filler hose, eh? Just as I kind of figured in the first place."

"You were kinda right, I guess."

"Well, I'm sure glad you finally fixed it. How much will it set me back?"

"Nothing yet. We don't have the part."

"What?"

"We don't have it in stock. We ordered one."

"So you haven't fixed it."

"Didn't say we did. Just told you we found the problem."

"How long will it take?"

"'Bout a week."

"Why so long?"

"It's rare. It's just not a thing we ever see. Somehow it seems to have got nicked way up inside. What've you been doing with this car, anyway?"

"Nothing. Just driving. Maybe it was defective in the first place."

"Anyway. It's all fouled up. We gotta get you a new one."

"What am I supposed to do in the meantime?"

"You'll just have to drive less."

"Great."

"We tried to wrap some tape onto it. Should hold it for now ..."

Later in the week I was driving along with Sally. We'd had dinner. Watched a movie.

She wanted to see my place. "A house in the suburbs. How domestic."

"Yeah. Don't know if I'll keep it, though."

"Hey, the 'burbs are comfy."

She was being sweet, Sally was. But my house was twenty klicks away, there wasn't much gas, and I hadn't planned on having an accomplice when next I tried a high-risk fuelling manoeuvre. Nevertheless, with Sally—oblivious to the situation—sitting beside me, I pulled into a station. The far pump was dimly lit and sloped perfectly away from the pay-booth.

I turned to her, tense, and smiled. "We're nearly out."

"Then we'd need a fill-up, wouldn't we?"

"I've been having some mechanical trouble. It might be a few minutes."

"Do you need help?"

"Oh heck no. You just stay in the car."

"I will."

I theorized that the split in the filler hose was only on one side or the other. If I jockeyed the nozzle right I might be able to stream gas away from the nick and avoid overt spillage. I'd have to experiment to find out. I only needed a few litres.

But no. After only a dozen seconds the sound and smell of so much gas pouring from under the car unnerved me. I stopped pumping and looked around to see if anyone was watching. The place was beautifully austere. Sally sat forward in the passenger seat, the overhead light on, browsing through a magazine. The attendant was nowhere in evidence, the lone light in the booth the only indication someone was even on duty. I was pretty well alone. I began to pump again.

The gas rivered down the pavement and laked into a shimmering basin several metres away in the dark. Were it not for the stench I could imagine by the undulation of light on the body of wet that it was a placid cove somewhere, or a good fishing spot nobody knew about. The fumes got strong. I got woozy for a second and shook my head. My brain felt shrunken.

Then the sound of the engine ticking away its heat jolted me alert. So much flammable liquid so close to hot metal. An image arose of the blaze I would author. I could not stop projection in the cinema of my mind; an encompassing blossom of orange fire; the panic, fumbling attempts at releasing the car door; screams; the beating of moist fists against a clouding car window. I suffered the whole smoke-shrouded attempt—Sally terrorized and suffocating—and measured in my mind how much damage I would allow to my own body in the struggle.

At what point could I morally save myself?

I unflexed my hand on the nozzle and carefully slid it back into its bracket.

I pulled the receipt from the credit card slot and slipped back into the car, careful of where I was stepping.

"What have you been doing out there?" Sally grimaced. "Pouring it on the ground?"

"Well, it's a long sad story …"

When we got to my place, Sally asked why she could smell gasoline again.

"Because there's a refinery in the hills back of here and when the wind is right—or wrong—it sends a lot of vapour our way."

"It's pretty bad."

"You get used to it after a while."

"I don't know if I could."

"I didn't know either, at first. Then I did some reading up on it."

"You did?" Sally smiled in her sweetest way. We were sitting on the couch, drinking wine. "What did you learn?"

"It's technical as hell, and I'm not sure I took it all in. But it has to do with different hydrocarbons and things like that. Mostly, I wanted to understand what those ugly metal pipe-towers are for."

"What are they for?"

"Distillation. They call them fractionating towers. They heat up the crude. Which is dense and lumpy and full of dirt a lot of the time. And feed it into the lower part of the system. The various molecules rise and condense at various levels. Or something like that. There's a bunch of physics and chemistry involved. To make gasoline they have to add hydrogen and some other stuff. Sometimes—based on the raw materials they're working with, where they're from, what's the grade and so on—they don't exactly know what end products will turn up and in what quantities. Often natural gas. Occasionally heavy oil. Whatever it is, it's always smelly if the wind is in our direction. But that's always kind of made it okay for me, you know? The idea they're working away over there making what they make but they never know for sure how it'll turn out. But once you get to know roughly what's going on you tend to tolerate it more. In my case, anyway."

Soon after that, Sally and I went to bed.

Driving back next morning we ran out of gas on the freeway.

"Didn't you fill up last night?"

"Yeah, well. As I said, that's the long and sad story. There's a problem with the fuelling."

"Why didn't you say so? We could have gone to my place."

"It doesn't matter. But I'm glad to hear you say that."

"I'm going to be late for work."

Fractionating

I got a ride to a gas station and then another ride back. It only took forty minutes. I was surprised it didn't take longer. Sally waited in the car. I poured the gas in carefully and put the can in the trunk, then slumped back into the driver's seat.

Sally didn't seem overly angry but sniffed the air. "I smell gas again."

"Jeez, really? I was good and careful."

"You got some on your pant leg."

She was right.

"Be careful, okay?"

"I will."

"Don't go near any open flame."

"I'll be particularly circumspect about that."

Sally sighed. "This kind of weirds me out …"

"Oh?" I was driving and dreading. "Aside from all the petro pollution that lingers as if we were aboard a beached tanker, how so?"

"All this bad smell in your car and at your house …" She hadn't laughed at my humour attempt, not even a smile. "But we had a nice time and you're such a nice guy."

"Glad you think so."

"I mean … Last night was cool and everything."

"It certainly was. I liked it a lot." We were silent a full minute. "But …" I spoke with my eyes on the road trying to think clearly, hoping the fuel supply would hold out, desiring with great urgency that Sally be delivered to work without further damage to her mood.

She was staring at me. "Should we have a relationship or not?"

"I don't know. Uh. It's not a question I'd ask myself."

"No." She turned away. "I guess I wouldn't either."

"I mean. There's you and me, basic components. How about we just see how things go?"

She smiled. "That sounds right."

"Gas again." Rodney came sniffing into my office. "I half-expect to find dead birds in here."

I was through with the telephone book and had the computer going full blast, trying to find a parts warehouse.

"You get with Sally last night?"

"Never mind."

"Good man!"

Without even looking at him I didn't like his smile.

"Forget about me ..." I turned from the screen. "What are you gonna do?"

Rod swung himself into a chair.

Later on I stood watching the mechanics puzzle. They scratched their heads, trying to fill my gas tank. The new part didn't make any difference at all. The gas poured out like it didn't care.

The sight did not bother me. I realized that I was feeling different. There was a detachment, something oddly new, indefinable but well-feeling. Ultimately it came down to the fact that I don't mind the smell of gas.

WOOD MOUNTAIN

On a dusty afternoon in Wood Mountain, Saskatchewan, summer of 1966, there was no reason for my cousin Edie to rear up and kick me.

But that's what she did. Just lunged out from a family huddle and shoved a foot into my mid-section—kick-boxer style—in plain view of Uncle David and Aunt Juliet, the cousins, my folks, brother and sister, everybody. We had been visiting their farm. I can't remember doing anything offensive. We were just kids.

Throughout the sixties, Dad took us on summer trips to the prairies. Nearly all our relatives were there. Most of them still lived out on the land, either in wind-wracked farmhouses or mean little paint-blistered bungalows within the thistle-garlanded towns. It was and still is a good three-day road trip from the coast of British Columbia to the flatlands of southern Saskatchewan in a family car loaded with children and supplies, but Dad loved to drive. He always owned some kind of stolid American sedan to get us across the three provinces in torrid late-July and deliver us back in time to play on the beach the last few weeks before school. Although the cars did their jobs, invariably by mid-trip they would require something retuned, rebuilt, remounted, or replaced. The relatives always had a garage with hoists, grease guns, welder, ratchet wrenches, plugs, points, coils and condensers, and spare parts either on hand or readily available. Mechanicing was a form of hospitality in our family. At some point during a visit it was a sure thing work would be done on the cars, whether they needed it or not.

Several of my uncles served in World War II, which was ironic because aside from the fact they were Saskatchewan farm boys, by heritage, temperament, language and culture down to their cabbage roll cuisine they were as Teutonic as the Kaiser (which, incidentally, was the name of one branch of the family). Uncle David was a motor pool sergeant with the 1st Armoured Brigade. He fought with a wrench in his hand across the Strait of Messina and up the boot past Naples to the street fighting in Ortona. Then on past Rome and Florence and clear up to Turin, almost as far as Austria—where he could have looked up relatives if it hadn't have been for, as he terms it, "da stupid war"—then looped back over the water to Holland and into Germany and nearly all the way to Berlin. Having endured years of danger and privation Uncle David—nobody ever called him Dave—survived to slide many times under Dad's '62 Acadian or '64 Comet or '67 Beaumont and declare, "Looks like your oil pan is buggert," or "You needa lube on dose ball joints," or "When'd you last flush da rad?"

But the point is that my cousin Edie, who was a kid of maybe seven at the time, just rose up and assaulted me as we were standing by the car saying goodbye. She led with her right sandal. I barely saw it coming. I stumbled backward, shocked but not hurt. Edie stepped deftly back into her family fold, nostrils flaring like a riled pit bull, her eyes coldly luminescent. She displayed neither fear nor hysteria, only blatant personal offence.

Though at age thirteen I'd had enough schoolyard tussles to understand what it was to get sucker-punched, it was still the most spontaneous, frightening, and unintelligible attack I'd ever suffered. No one missed the quickness of it, the frozen efficiency of its execution, or its disturbing manifestation of physical non sequitur. The gathering plummeted silent as if nerve-gassed.

And all this after a quality two-day visit loaded with the traditional warm offerings: sit-down meals, countryside drives, pasture picnics. We shared quality child-adventure on the austere hillsides outside town: herding cows, chasing gophers, and firing bullets from a rusty .22 into the slough, the impacts bringing curling rock-sized moils of brown and green murk rolling to the surface. Edie was quietly with us through the whole familial-bonding experience. But she stung me good anyway. In the car as we were leaving my mother was quiet. Dad too. The other kids snickered. Nobody asked what I thought.

Two-and-a-half decades years later my telephone rang too early one morning and the voice on the line said: "It's your Aunt Juliet in Regina."

"Well hi. This is a surprise. How are you doing?"

"Pretty bad, but that's not why I called. Your cousin Edie just moved out to Vancouver. I want you to keep an eye on her."

"Good grief. Edie from Wood Mountain?"

"Nobody's lived at Wood Mountain for years. She was last at Calgary but some business with a man drove her out."

It developed that Aunt Juliet did not have trust in her daughter's ability to fend for herself outside the protective social structure of a prairie community. Maybe not even then. Since I was the only one of the clan living in the coastal metropolis other than, now, Edie herself, it came shortly to pass that I dialed a number at an advertising and promotions company and left a message for her to call me.

Two weeks later my phone again rang too early in the morning.

"This is Edie Wallenco." The voice was duskier but I recognized clipped syllables from a long-ago distance. "Did you leave a message?"

"Uh, yeah." I rued, in my head-dullness, not having a better opener. "Weeks ago."

"That's unfortunate. To be honest with you, I did not know who you might be. I miscalculated that there might be family here."

"Gee, that's an odd way of putting it, but ... Didn't you recognize the family name?"

"There are more than a dozen Wallenco's in the phone book. Do you think we are related to all of them?"

"Uh. No ... I don't know."

"Of course not."

"How do you know?"

"I ran a search. It took some time."

"Whoo-ee."

"You never can be too careful."

"I guess not. Anyway, gosh. It's been a thousand years."

"Actually it's been exactly twenty-six years, ten months, and a few weeks."

"Oh. You keep careful records."

"How did you find my workplace?"

"Aunt Juliet ... your mom called. She wants me to spy on you."

"Oh ..." Her sigh hissed like steam over the phone. "She's become quite a pest."

"I didn't know. Sorry."

We met for lunch downtown. She was wearing a hat. A great big floppy thing. During this particular year not one other person in all of North America—male or female—was wearing a hat. Her look was as bizarre as if she had been swinging a hoop skirt and waving a lace parasol.

"I'm trying to lose weight." She sat after shaking hands without otherwise introducing herself. "I'll only have salad and a little wine."

I was single in those days. Off and on. Dating like crazy; having lots of short, sharp, sometimes nasty entanglements. Through it all I'd become a seasoned luncher and from the first moment with Edie it was uncomfortably manifest between us that this was far too much like a date for comfort. I felt it and was sure she did by her nervous chatter. Then, in twenty minutes, she drank three glasses of Pinot blanc. Redness came across her face.

"I should tell you I left Calgary because Kenneth was cheating on me."

"Kenneth?"

"My boyfriend."

"That's too bad."

"He was a jerk …" She let the sentence hang, fingering her wineglass, salad untouched.

I debated what to do. That morning while planning what to talk about I had considered inviting her to Paul's place for the usual collected *caballero* weekend fete.

She stared at me as if I should have known about Kenneth.

"So. How long did you live in Calgary?"

"One guy." She spoke as if not having heard me. "All those years."

"A lot of years?"

"Many many."

"And now you're out here."

"The company offered me a lateral."

"What is it you do, exactly?"

"Everything."

"You work at an ad agency?"

"We do everything. Yeah."

"Did you go to school anywhere?"

"I did a couple of years at SAIT."

"SAIT?"

"Southern Alberta Institute of Technology. I had to leave." She took a drink. "It was … yech."

"Yech?"

"Uh-huh." She finished her wine. "You know."

"Well, I …"

"Are you going to drink that?" Edie pointed to my half-glass.

"Absolutely." I took it up and drank.

She stared at me seriously.

I smacked my lips as a comic gesture. "Isn't it absurd about Aunt Juliet?"

Edie darkened. "How do you mean?"

"Her instructions to me. To keep an eye on you."

"That's not absurd."

I did not have a comeback. "Oh." I drank the rest of my wine. "Okay."

"I take it you have no family responsibilities."

"Um … In what sense?"

"Over the years I've heard about it. Big city lifestyle. Some kind of adventure-ish job involving insurance fraud. Left your wife and child. Lots of girlfriends. Trips all over the place. You don't look after your brothers and sister. You seldom see your parents."

"I wouldn't say that."

"What would you say?"

"I …" The loadedness of her challenge weighed on me and hardened something inside. "Look. There's a reason we haven't seen each other since 1966."

Edie's eyes narrowed. "Do tell."

"I turned fourteen the next year and worked the summer on a farm outside Swift Current so didn't go on vacation with the family. I helped pull down an old barn and learned to drive and helped out with the barley harvest. The next year I was working in a department store and the year after that I was marching around a parade square at Camp Borden. After that I was old enough to go my own way so you never saw me again until now. Do you remember kicking me in the gut that time we were saying goodbye in Wood Mountain?"

Edie stared blankly. As I waited for her to say something it occurred to me that aside from the wine she might have been on some kind of mind-altering medication. We sat silent for a full minute. Her gaze was directed to the outside. She seemed to be daydreaming, and never answered my question.

I offered to pick up the cheque. Edie did not oppose. On the way out I helped her on with her coat. At the door, standing aside for others to enter, she leaned unnecessarily against me. I could not tell what this was.

After discussion with Paul—wherein I assured him that if she wasn't the most socially skilled person he'd ever meet then at least she was another female person he could add to his scant "possibles" list— Edie was issued and accepted an invitation. Due to my impressions of her over lunch we were careful to co-invite only our least confrontational friends, opting to sacrifice spontaneous humour and provocative subject matter in favour of placid conviality.

Edie arrived slightly after the appointed time and refused to take off her coat. It was a heavy, garishly mauve woollen thing that looked like an animal hide dyed horribly wrong. She did, however, let me take her hat.

Nor would she sit completely down. When offered a seat, she chose instead to perch on an arm of the couch, well away from anyone else. Eventually her hunched presence seemed to fill everyone—we'd procured a few of our A-list cohorts: Graham, a gay man working in the film industry; and Ian and Janet, who lived on a boat—with an odd anticipation.

She initially refused a drink.

"Can I get you something else?" Paul stood by and spoke softly to her. "A Coke? Mineral water?"

"Oh ..." Edie leaned and looked directly down into Paul's glass. "What have you got there?"

"Wine. Chardonnay something or other."

"I wasn't going to, but ..."

"Can I get you a small glass?"

"Small as can be, please."

For the rest of the evening we did not see her small glass go empty. If it wasn't Paul seeing to everybody, it was Graham sportingly topping her up from his own bottle, or me seeing that she was having a good time, or herself leaning over and gripping whatever might be in the ice bucket to help herself.

We talked and ate and drank. Edie seemed especially enamoured of Graham, who regaled us with stories of celebrities and their idiosyncratic commonplaces. At one point I noted the permanence of her hand on his arm and could not miss the mild pain showing on his face.

It was well along but not too late when Ian and Janet began to take their leave and Graham jumped up along with them, claiming an early call. Edie lolled on the couch while Paul and I said our goodbyes. When we turned back to her she was in the giddy act of flinging off her shoes. One of them hit Paul's favourite Wyeth print and left a mark on the open field scene just below the lonely house. I could tell by his lack of panic that he was attracted to her.

Taking the cue, I left the room and started on the dishes. After twenty minutes, with all but the pot scrubbing done, I checked on them. They were huddled on the floor by the fire. Paul had put on some Pat Metheny.

"You guys need a drink?" I spoke before noticing Paul's hand at Edie's face, the gentle way he was brushing hair from her eyes. I backed away and made for the Brillo pad.

The lack of sound from the living room was nearly disconcerting, but as I wiped dry the last of the cookware and gently placed it back into Paul's kitchen cupboards I reasoned that they might be getting along handsomely in a non-verbal sort of way. I tiptoed back toward the living room. They were still by the fire, Edie now reposed in Paul's arms.

As I tried to pass by without looking, Paul turned up his face and gestured. I stopped and looked at Edie. Her eyes were sealed shut.

I shrugged. "Guess she's asleep."

"More like passed out."

I noticed now that Paul did not seem all that comfortable, despite the doubtless thrill of getting some close contact with a female for the first time in at least a year. We paused to hear her slight snore.

I crouched beside them. "What do you want to do?"

"Stand up straight, for starters." Paul began to extricate himself.

"Can you handle things?"

"I suppose."

"Should we wake her?"

"We could try."

Paul finished removing himself and I whipped a pillow off the sofa to support Edie's head. Then, as Paul stood by, I tried to shake her to consciousness. No go. She sighed heavily. I caught the full boozy blast, even though I had been drinking too. "I think she's just gonna have to sleep it off."

Paul arranged cushions on the couch. "Let's get her over here."

Edie slumbered solidly as we made the transfer. Paul went for a blanket and covered her. He stood gazing. "She only looks a little bit like you."

"Are you kidding? Other than a last name, I share absolutely nothing in common with this babe."

"Oh, I don't know. A little of the face baggage."

"Face baggage?'

Paul traced a fingertip across the base of one of Edie's eyes. "See? Same discolouration. Likely allergic. Give her a few more years and she'll have your puffiness too."

"Oh go on!"

"She's definitely got the dipso traits."

"That's some ironic commentary coming as it does from a common drunkard like yourself."

"Me? Well, you're a souse."

"You're a tippler."

"Lush."

"Wet brain."

"Sot."

"Liquor-ite."

"Intoxicate."

"Inebriate."

"Wino."

"Sponge."

"Guzzler."

"Alky …"

I looked at the VCR clock. "Cripes, it's two o'clock in the morning! What are we gonna do with her?"

"Let her sleep." Paul straightened the cover over Edie. "I'll see she's okay."

"Thanks, man." I pulled on my jacket and looked at Edie once more. "She's my cousin but I don't know her."

"I guess not." Paul smiled. "She's odd."

"Good call." I made for the door. "'Night now."

"Good night." Paul turned off the lamp over Edie's cozy form.

In the morning I slept late and forgot to call and find out the situation. Paul phoned from the bar late in the afternoon. I could hear the din of the hockey game on the TV screens.

"Is she still on the couch?"

Paul laughed. "No."

"What happened?"

"Nothing. She left in the night. I didn't see her."

"Just took off?"

"Yup."

"No note?"

"No nothing."

"Well I guess she might have been disoriented. Man, I sure hope she wasn't driving."

"I have a feeling she wasn't."
"I better give her a call."
"Maybe tomorrow."
"Yeah. That'll be discreet."
"She seems like a good kid. I'd like to get to know her better."
"Don't say stuff like that, Paul."
"You're right ..."

But I forgot to call the next day. Four days later I thought of it, then reconsidered, thinking she might be feeling weird about being left unspoken-to for half a week. I decided to debate the question with Paul. I saw him the next night.
"What? You mean you haven't called her yet?"
"I didn't get around to it."
"I don't know. It might be too late now."
"Don't be silly. We're cousins. We don't owe each other any kind of protocol."
"I don't know. You owe each other something."
"What do you think that is?"
"Search me." Paul went back to his drink.

The next day, driving and thinking, I resolved to call Edie that weekend and invite her to the bar with Paul and me. But plans changed and we ended up going up country to a hobby ranch that one of our bar buddies owns. The next weekend was Thanksgiving and a few weeks later the Grey Cup party and then there were other things. Christmas and New Year's. I kept forgetting to call her. Months went by. After a while I hardly thought of her.

Eight years later, my dad died.

The only relatives to come out for the funeral were Uncle David, walking cane in hand, with one of his countless grandchildren—whose name I was told several times and which I forgot immediately on each occasion—as an escort. We were surprised he showed up, having just lost Aunt Juliet the previous winter.

At the house after the service I sat on the arm of my uncle's chair. "So glad you could come, Uncle David."

"What else would I do?"

"It's a long way. Travelling can be a pain."

Uncle David waved a hand.

"You're a tough guy, nonetheless. No wonder Hitler didn't stand a chance."

"Hah ha!" Uncle David's laughter held too much mirth and not enough irony. "Yah, we give it to him good."

"No kidding."

"But never mind. What you doing dese days?"

"I'm researching a history of the Italian campaign. I was wondering, now that you're here, if you have any memories I could record."

Uncle David waved his hand again. "It was just a stupid ting."

"I guess you were glad to get back after all those years."

"I like farming da best. And raising our children."

"How's Edie? I haven't heard from her in years."

"Edie? My my." Uncle David smiled. "She's in Winnipeg. Married a good man."

"Oh yeah? That's great."

"And how are you doing?"

"I'm great. Doing this history book project, as I say."

Uncle David was quiet.

"Driving a good car." I felt I needed to add that.

"And for your family?"

I nodded my head toward the side of the room where my sister and brothers clustered about my mother. "As you see."

"Where are your little ones?"

"Well ... I'm not married."

"Oh?"

"I was. But now I'm not."

"Ah ..." Uncle David smiled. "You know, our Edie, she's doing pretty good."

"We saw each other ..." I avoided Uncle David's eyes. "Years ago. She looked ... happy."

"You know she makes two hundred tousand a year at dat advertising business."

"No!"

"She does. Squirrels it away. Her and her husband and children. Lives quiet and modest."

"I find that amazing."

"She was always a quiet one."

"Quiet or not, I find it staggering that she makes such a good dollar. I asked what she did one time and she kind of just shrugged me off."

Uncle David sat silent. I waited for him to tell me Edie was a big-time executive, a creative co-coordinator; producer, high-flight sales rep, maybe a CEO. But nothing. He just kept smiling.

I looked away. Soon I was daydreaming into a reminiscence of all those prairie road trips. Little places with geographic names like Swift Current, Maple Creek, and Grande Prairie, or long-dead settler christenings like Glenbain and Kincaid and Lefleche. Practical appellations that represented the loci of who-knew-how-many agricultural lives—grain tenders, machine sellers, part fixers, reed-between-the-teeth talkers—places which, by now, were tumbleweed barren, most of them having started to fall apart shortly after my last trip with the family. I had heard that only a few persons remained in some of them. When we visited Dad's friends on a farm near Kincaid, the place had been thriving. But a recent magazine article I'd seen discussing the decline of the grain-farming economy profiled it as a ghost town. The hotel kitchen was the last business still open, around the back of the once proud three-storey building; a photo showed the front of the place boarded up. I imagined lonesome, dirty streets and off-kilter grain elevators ready for dynamite or the arsonist.

I snapped out of my reverie when Uncle David swept his arms around to indicate an appreciation for the dozens of friends and family in the house. "Your father liked to see all da relatives."

"He never forgot he was from Saskatchewan."

"You should see it now. Much easier to live. Family all around."

"Man, I really gotta figure out how to get out there and visit all of you guys."

"I'm past eighty." Uncle David's smile faded. "Don' leave it too long."

"I'll try not to."

But I was referring to the decision, not necessarily the trip. In fact I knew instantly, as Uncle David turned away, that I would have little need to go that way again.

CIRCUMSPECTION MAN

We used the same bank of elevators and were often going places at the same time. Each ride let me quip a convivial "Some rain, huh?" or "You again?" Over the weeks the familiarity momentum bounded toward a lunch, maybe.

One day as the doors paused at her floor I came out and asked.

"Oh ... I hardly get time ..."

"Dinner, perhaps."

A wide smile. "That would be better." She stepped off the car looking back at me.

So on a Friday late afternoon in a suitable new place near the office we were smiling at each other across a table.

"Glad you could make it." I'd only had to wait four minutes.

"I had nothing planned."

"Lucky for me."

"And it's good you didn't want to put it off until, like, eight o'clock like some people do." She beamed, perusing her menu. "I'm so hungry by five."

The clock behind the ferns by the bar said it was five-twenty. "Well for goodness sake, girl, order."

She beamed. "I'm kind of taken with the animal designs on this menu."

"I thought you might."

"Really?"

"From what I've gathered about you. All those elevator rides."

"You're being silly."

"No, no, look close. They're a non-threatening cartoonized iconography of human domination." I set my pupils into hers. "We enjoy an artistic rendering of nature's variety, cutesy images of creatures cavorting, which neutralizes any or all tendency toward revulsion when we eat them. Makes denial dead easy. Perfect for those of us who want to at least pretend we're concerned about the environment while chomping away on animals produced by ecologically disastrous Franken-farming."

"How does that relate to us in the elevator?"

"I heard you once talk about conservation."

"I remember. But that's quite a stretch. From a general interest in ecology to a mini-screed on human corporeal iconography."

"I took a chance."

"So. Hah ha. You're a graphic designer with attitude."

"I'm an account rep who reads *Mother Jones*. Or used to, anyway."

"Used to?"

"It got boring. All that pure-hearted earnest-itude. Then I heard my name might be on some kind of subversive list just for subscribing—only in the States, mind you—but what the heck. I mean, you don't want Homeland Security after you for any reason, right? Then I realized I don't care. At least nobody's tried to throw me off a plane." I paused, joyous at how easy it was all coming. "I'm still an account rep, though ..."

She smiled.

I examined the menu. "The fawns are a little too 'nursery,' aren't they? Kind of over-cute. Why couldn't they have used a few ticked-off monkeys?"

"Ooh, primates. That would freak me."

"Really?"

"Too cannibal."

"Good point."

Together, we looked at the specials list, me holding the big page sideways between us. I saw that she was sneaking a view of me whenever she could.

"Do I disgust you?"

"You do look slightly maniacal."

"Only when I'm happy."

"Hmm. That suggests all kinds of terrible things but I'm so hungry I think I'll ignore further exploration of your character in favour of ordering something to eat. The fish in this place is supposed to be great."

"That's why we're here."

"I think I've decided on the shad. And the salad special they describe with these Italian words."

"*Molto bene?*"

"No, no ..." She read. "*Verde al fresco.*"

"Sounds fine."

"What does it mean?"

"Fresh leafy things, I reckon."

"No, no. The other thing."

"The something that sounded like Eggs Benny?"

"Yes."

"*Molto bene.* The only Italian words I know. Means very good."

She shrugged. "I'm the adventuresome type only rarely."

"Necessity or disposition?"

"Both."

"Is it okay if I go for the sole?"

She seemed surprised. "Why ask?"

"I guess I sought your attitude toward spirituality." I chuckled, then shrugged. "And I can't resist even the cheapest pun."

"Oh. Sole. I get it."

"It's lame, I admit."

"Alas." She sighed, mock-ironic. "Maybe this kind of weird verbal self-amusement should be predictable in a sales rep …"

I smiled wide as I could.

"… But sure, it's okay with me if you go for the soul."

"Check."

"Not so fast. It irks me to see that you don't know what form of sole or soul I was referring to."

"Oof. You got me."

She looked again at her menu. "Everything looks good. It's only shellfish that bothers me."

"Can't stand the idea of eating what amounts to insects of the sea?"

"No, allergies. Anaphylactic reaction."

"What's that?"

"My throat swells up. I can't breathe. I die."

"Wow."

"It only happens once in a while."

"Hmm …" I frowned heavily enough to cover both humour and genuine concern. "Must be embarrassing."

"Yes, it is." She gazed at me earnestly. "So, in a way, it's entirely appropriate that we check with each other about what we eat."

"Just call me Circumspection Man."

"Right. Whatever you say …"

"Okay, okay. A little over the top. So I won't dash off and change into my cape and tights."

"Please don't bother on my account at least." She looked around. Our server was nowhere in sight. "Meanwhile, I hope you don't mind ordering while I'm in the ladies' room."

"Not at all."

I studied only so much of the glory of her walking away—not flashily undulating, but confidently female enough to enthral—so as to maintain a genteel standard aspired to mainly in my own mind. This same mind then ranged for its singular pleasure to the likely structure of the evening: Dinner—ordered at five-thirty, according to the fern clock—would take the minimum required time. The place was not busy. Two good hours of conversation, a walk along the seawall, perhaps. One hour. That put it around nine. We might speak briefly outside her place. Shake hands or peck cheeks good night. Damn enjoyable, respectful, non-aggressive cheery date.

Then time enough to get home and watch some TV.

All things being level—if I didn't blow it, if the restaurant roof didn't cave in, if we didn't get hit by a truck crossing the street, if we didn't discuss religion and she turned out to be a believer or something equally as unbalanced—this would be money in the bank. Plenty of potential; lots of good times pointing straight like desert highway into unimpeded infinity.

I tried not to be smiling too densely when she returned.

"They have such cool washrooms."

"Just for you, my dear. I checked all that out."

She laughed.

The wine arrived. I did not taste, but performed my customary swill-around, smell, smile, and gestured approval for the pour.

She held out her glass. "You're kind of an expert, aren't you?"

"At wine?"

"At hanging out. Asking girls for dates. Finding tony places to eat. Making sharp and funny and practiced conversation. And yes, sniffing at wine like it was nothing."

"Well thanks." I worked up my best semi-pensive look. "I like to think it's not just boredom."

"I wouldn't say it couldn't be. It looks like it could get that way."

"You just suggested I was an expert, though. Doesn't that make it kind of ... noble?"

"Kind of an expert. A bored kind of expert. Certainly better than a sportsman, though. That's for absolutely sure. But as for noble ... we'll see."

I studied her overt gaze. Hands. Arms. Up my shoulders. It made me self-conscious.

"You're frisking me."

"You don't wear a watch?"

"Haven't for years."

"It must be awkward. Business-wise, at least."

"Not at all. There are clocks everywhere if you think about it. There are radios playing in every car and cab, blaring the time every few minutes. There are TVs in every bar tuned to cable news with the time in several zones on constant display. Computer screens the world over scroll the clock. There's the Gastown Steam Whistle shrilling it up every fifteen minutes. There's the Noon Horn down at the harbour blaring the first four notes of 'O Canada.' Stanley Park has the Nine O'clock Gun. There's the sun that comes up once a day and tells me it's morning. When I get hungry, I eat, denoting breakfast, lunch, and suppertime. I get sleepy when I'm tired. Usually after the sun goes down.

"It's good to be aware of time passing, you know. I mean, if I have an appointment I take extra care to leave in time to get there. I have to time the walk, the subway, bus, cab, whatever. It puts my feet on the ground. Not having a wristwatch is a way of being in touch. Of knowing what's going on with myself." I drank. "Sometimes I get tired, though."

"Whoa, non sequitur!"

"Sorry. What was I talking about?"

"Well first it was this cool survey about the ubiquity of time and the various ways it's displayed. Then there was a colourful survey of various clock sites around the city. Some kind of statement about human innate chronological awareness ... Then suddenly you were getting tired of something."

"Oh, yeah."

"Were you just BS-ing?"

"That's not nice."

"Go on with what you were saying."

"I was finished."

"Darn. Just when I was beginning to fall for it."

"Fall for what? The clocks?"

"It was fascinating. Your recitation and voice modulation were kind of creating this Zen-like verbal induction that I was finding sexy."

"Whoa ..."

"Don't worry. I didn't take it as naked seduction talk."

"I should hope not."

"Fully clothed seduction talk, more like."

"Yeow! I've got to be damn careful what I say to you."

"Feel free to do so."

"Okay ..." Despite my elation at surviving her disconcertingly accurate observational salvo, I was desperate to finish my thought. "But as for the found-clock business, it's my thing only. I don't know anybody else who does it. I think it only works for me."

"I hope for the sake of your career and the sake of all us tardiness-intolerant career women that it does."

We both took a drink.

I decided to strive ahead. "You're pretty cool."

"How do you mean?"

"You handle yourself with ... aplomb. You're immediate. Sharp. Alert."

"Thank you."

Her smile was laden. I took a moment to savour my view across the table and figure where next to boldly go.

"What, if I may be so cold"—I hardened my face—"is your internal mien?"

"What are you talking about? Cold?"

"You heard me."

"I try never to be ... mean." She grinned. "To anybody."

I mock-grimaced. *"Touché."*

"Thought you'd like that."

"I do."

When the food came I forced myself to chew slowly. "Okay, cliché time." I paused, glass in hand, and regarded her. "If you could change anything you wanted to change in the world, what would you change?"

"That lady's perfume over there." She rolled her eyes at a freshly seated foursome.

I couldn't help but frown at her parry. Then, looking at her, I knew I'd made an even bigger mistake. She saw my expression and at the same time I understood that she was legitimately perturbed.

"It's bugging you?"

She reached for her purse. "Among my complications ..." She rummaged and held up an inhaler. "Asthma."

She administered a quick-fingered twist of the instrument—a deft insertion into mouth and the audible suck of medicated vapour. She sat deadened for a few seconds. Mouth closed. Breath purposeful. I had scarcely known where to look during the procedure. At the end of it, as she smiled again and met me in the eyes, I also noticed for certain the offending scent. It was a nasty musk drifting deadly at us, moist and florid as mouldy curtains.

"Man. That is powerful."

"I ..." She broke off into scraping audible breaths. Seconds passed. Her eyes reddened alarm. She whacked at her chest with an open hand and then a fist. "I ...!" She could not talk.

"Can I help in some way?" I dropped my napkin and put a hand on the back of my chair.

"No. No." She waved me still. "I ..." Coughing.

There was nothing to do but wait until the clatter abated. It was a long wait. Customers noticed us. The server did a swoop, a transparent check-out manoeuvre that further high-centred us as disrupters of the peace. She continued to have trouble and motioned that she would deal with it in the ladies' room.

When she was gone, the server came by, eyeing the table unenthusiastically, offering no further assistance.

Then once left alone again I had the distinct sensation that I had become invisible. It took a considerable amount of time to get some attention. I gestured to the half-consumed meals. "Put these in a bag, would you please?" The server immediately started to collect the plates. "And gimme the check when you get a chance." I was not offered a dessert.

Less than a minute later I was heaping money onto a chrome plate. During all this action she never reappeared.

I sat for ten minutes with the doggy bags in front of me, then went and took up a station outside the ladies' room. Straining, I could hear little within, only the suggestion of a cough. When a middle-aged woman with an enormous handbag stepped past me, eyes averted, touching the door, I acknowledged an impulse to ask her to check on my date, but opted, in the three-quarters of a second available, not to. I measured things intently for several minutes. Defining my position. Timing for the return of the big handbag-woman—whom I thought I could hear closing a stall door. Opening again. Washing. Blow-drying. Then the silence of a hair-comb session. It was when I knew she would re-emerge in one second, inevitably re-seeing me standing there furtive and preoccupied in the hall, that the craven imagery of it all crumbled my insides.

Before the door could open—with a dispatch borne of raw embarrassment—I was gone.

In the cab the hockey game was on the radio. I asked the driver to turn it off, not wanting to know the score. All the way home I was calculating that if there wasn't too much traffic, and no police sobriety roadblock on the bridge, and no other haphazard exigency to slow things up, I'd be home in time to watch the second period.

Hockey. Yes. That was where my presence was now. Away from the evening. Excused from conversation or contemplating true confession or reverting to bluntness or super-tact. No need for discussion of relationship distress, fast-forward sexual flirtation or brow-furrowed forewarnings of familial complications. All of it was just silly stage business in comparison to the rink contest. The ice-borne debacle of players with blades on their feet. Sticks in their hands. Velocity at their headings. Rifling the dangerous disk in an endless feature of shot upon shot upon shot upon shot.

At home it was the last minute of the first period, Rangers and Canucks. I watched respectfully. It was as important as anything.

KITTY

That year my castle was a studio under a three-story brownstone with good access to bars, music, and public transit. In back was the kitchen/eating area where I had my desk. There was the bathroom; razor, comb, soap, and nail-clippers by the taps on the sink. At the rear was a closet area large enough to be a sleeping space. My bed was a low futon you could fold into a couch if you wanted to. I never wanted to. The telephone lay on the floor within arm's reach. There was no other furniture. In idle moments I'd stand at either of the windows and look up at birds in trees or spy on the feet and legs that cadenced by on the sidewalk. It was cozy and hidden and all mine.

Wine in the fridge. Snacks. Cocktail shaker.

Just what I always wanted. Needless to say, I entertained a lot of women. Aside from working like a madman during the day and drinking six or seven Jack Manhattans per night I made sure there was little else to do.

I ate out a lot. The office was ten minutes away by bus so I didn't need a car. I would shower at night and dry off with my one towel. I enjoyed the body warmth under a duck-down quilt and the contrasting coolness across my face. Alone in the dark—despite the thrumming, troubled world that was lowly sounding through the masonry walls about me—my contentment was titanic.

The only weirdness was that a number of cats had invited themselves in over the months. The place had a good-sized main room I would have preferred to keep empty, but in the corner by a window a ragged pile was building up with boxes from a former situation. I liked to keep one window open at least a crack, even in cold weather.

They would duck cautiously through onto the high sill, investigating the drop. Sometimes they chanced it, other times they opted to pick their perspicacious way down the dicey box ladder. Most only stayed a few minutes, long enough to find out there was no food and the sole human inhabitant wasn't willing to leave his futon to give them the merest pat on the head.

One morning as I awoke in the grey early light a couple of cats sat watching me. Emerging from dream-state, for an instant I thought them porcelain. Sphinxian stare-creatures, still and stern. They seemed not the least concerned at my stirring.

One was a long-haired cutie—copper coloured—with subtle whitish striping. I thought it was a she-cat by the neatness of her fur and perfect tail placement about her body. She was founded pertly on clenched bottom, staring me through with cold interest but just soft enough about it to be polite. The other one—a bullish silver tabby with markings so distinct the characteristic forehead 'M' appeared tattooed—sat with such lofty assurance that I subliminally assigned it masculinity even though I never got the chance to see what was between its hind legs.

I smiled at the orange one. Her eyes narrowed and widened again and then avoided mine. She yawned and looked to where her partner was now nosing about the springy regions of my swivel chair, then further under the desk. He went out of sight rummaging in the storage carton where I kept scrap paper.

My sentry turned back to me but then her partner tipped the box over—it plopped loudly, spilling slippery magazines across the floor—shocking her to arched alertness. They meowed to each other one time, then, in unison, moved away from the bedside and continued their patrol. A wander-about in the kitchen. Nosings at the garbage can and stove. A gentle sidle back to the centre of the apartment. They stood. Sat. Mewled softly to each other. Stood, wandered, sat again.

The clock by my head read 6:10. Another hour at least before getting up. I turned to the wall and closed my eyes. A noise woke me in time to see a grey tail levitate through the window and disappear. There was a faint scratching sound somewhere out of sight. I slept again.

The rasp of violent claw-work got my eyes open and focused just as the orange cat leapt from a teetering box she had been traversing. She did the acrobatic moves necessary to land upright and stood on the hardwood with claws clenched, looking acidly up at the stack of cartons. The column teetered from the wall and fell like a reaching arm toward the feline. She dodged, wailing, hightailing it from the noise and scatter of my packed-up books, kitchen things, clothes, keepsakes, and the trumpet I had kept since high school (never played but always kept). She scrabbled along the floor in a straight line for me. Our eyes locked, I had a moment of fear. But she merely galloped the last few feet—ears tensed low—and vanished under the futon frame, an orangey disappearing blur across my sleep-thickened consciousness.

I was momentarily astounded at her magic trick, sure that the scant clearance between the floor and the bottom of the frame wouldn't let a mouse flee into there, let alone a cat. But she disappeared anyhow.

In the calm of morning, with the fallen boxes still and the noise thus abated, I remained in bed, propped on an elbow, contemplating what I might best do.

I peered over the side of the futon, shielding my face with a hand in case of a panicked lashing, contacting the cool floor with my forehead. Nothing was visible beneath the frame except lint and darkness. "Here, kitty."

I breathed and then sneezed into the ridiculous dust, cursing myself for being such a bachelor. There was no indication that either my call or nasal outburst had had any effect on the cat. In fact, it felt like I was alone again. I shook my head to make certain I was awake and wondered when my bourbon-with-vermouth nightly habit was going to make stuff like this—real or imagined, taken care of or ignored—reduce me to a groaning breakdown. A spell of dizziness lingered, then went away. I knew I was awake alright, if hungover. But try as I did in the silence of the morning with just the lightest hum of traffic outside and only the subtle ticking of the bedside clock marking a faint rhythm in my ears, I could hear nothing of the live creature below me.

I lay sighing back onto the bed. Gentle scrabbling from below, more sensed than heard. It went silent. What to do?

I had no inclination to reach into the murk and try to apprehend a clawed, anxious animal, no matter how small and cute. Crouching like a feline myself—stealthy as I imagined they saw themselves to be—I crabbed sideways off the bed and squatted low on the floor. With particular care I surveyed each possible cat opening below the bare two-by-fours of the frame. It occurred to me that the whole bed would have to be lifted to free the cat. I stood straight and reasoned that before I did anything I should get some clothes on. Vanity aside,

I could not banish the image of unsheathed claws and bared teeth launched in either aggression or play at the first available dangling object. The sticky-sharp pins at the ends of her paws. The gnashing needle-teeth. I pulled on a pair of sweatpants.

It had been near a half-year since I'd moved in. Just long enough to have forgotten how heavy a double futon and frame weighs. Especially if you've just gotten out of bed. I hefted once, let it back down to improve my grip, then heaved again. I held the bed aloft, not breathing, expecting maybe an orange bolt—a smoking cartoon bullet—to fly past my ankles and out.

This line of thought brought with it a brain-clearing of sorts, enough for me to understand that simply lifting the bed without creating a further escape route was not going to cure a frightened cat of agoraphobia. Sure enough, from what I could glimpse, the cringing kitty crouched pasted to the floor at the very far edge against the wall, glaring immobile. I held the bed for a few more seconds, then gently lowered it back down. I stabbed on slippers and threw a T-shirt over myself and went through the kitchen to the big room, unlocked the door and left it wide open.

I perched on the desk. The time was 6:56. A coffee would go good now was all my mind could produce. The cat did not appear, though the draft from the door would have penetrated even the furthest reaches of *Lower Futonia* to beckon the feline with its promise of freedom. I tried lifting the bed again. Nothing. It was now 7:05. Time to get going.

I closed the door and re-stacked the box-ladder to make an easy-for-a-cat-to-climb escape route to the window. Then I shucked my clothes and went for the bathroom, reasoning that if the kitty had any sense she would come out once alone and leave. For some odd reason

I sensed that, like me, she would have an instinct to move on.

Nine minutes later the phone rang. It was work. I took down some notes and hung up. Then I threw on underwear and slacks and shirt and socks and jacket. I got my briefcase together and made sure my iPod and cell phone were charged and planted at handy places on my person. I rushed out the door.

During the morning I thought no more of the cat. It was only at afternoon coffee when somebody in the office mentioned vet bills that I remembered my visitor. I remembered, then forgot again, remembered once more, then the cat left my mind completely.

Not that I had any idea at all about what I might do about her, preoccupied as I was. For weeks I'd been trifling with a recent hire named Wei. Smart. Serious. A twentysomething sweetheart who clerked in administration and with whom from the first I'd detected a glowing mutual spark. I planned to get her back to my refuge as soon as I could and had arranged a six p.m. date for drinks and dinner. Later on I walked her through an art exhibit.

Wei's English wasn't steady. I don't know a word of Cantonese and alas, my *forte* has always been repartee. Still, with a makeshift pidgin we conversed, nearly giggling with the effort it took to bottle the rampaging carnality burbling between us. I kept a light hand at the small of her back. She swept her hair across my cheek. At the gallery, in the back of a darkened video installation transmitting an endless loop of two guys fighting, reconciling, arguing, and fighting again, Wei let me kiss her.

Inside the door at my place we necked standing up and as soon as clothes could be shed occupied the bed. Though normally more a man of action than words in this situation, I inexplicably felt it flighty and entertaining to make small talk. I quickly mentioned the cat.

"Kitty?"

"Under the bed."

Her face annealed toward menace, a state rigidly conflicting with her condition of naked and my condition of being, just at that moment, poised to immerse. Thus I knew that before we could go on I would have to say something.

"It's gone, Wei." I spoke from the firm certainty that if I were the cat I most assuredly would be.

"Gun?"

"Uh-huh."

"Sure?"

"I'm sure, yes."

I knew that if this had been any other circumstance—if we were riding in a car or talking over a café table—I would have had to substantiate my answer. Here, I hoped I was excused.

But no. Things were not the same. The mere possibility of cat-under-bed seemed a tangible factor even as we resumed mutual movement. Intercourse morphed into a conjoined standoffish anomaly. My fingers rasped upon the mannequin indifference of her skin. Her refracted resolve to carry on manifested itself as an odd facial grimace neither erotic nor disdainful.

Thus, though we ground together in the accepted fashion, I struggled to concentrate, could not make my brain remain still and rid itself of the notion that if I were a cat I would be gone but that the cat was not me and I was not the cat. Moving inside Wei but thinking inside the feline, I nearly shuddered from the effort to detach and enjoy. Might the cat actually let fear and disorientation keep it in a dry tense place for who knew how long? Might I ever again enjoy Wei's perfect body after this ragingly imperfect coupling?

Still we proceeded.

I came—reflexes gripping—hollering a bit. Not inspired. Mostly by habit.

Wei mimicked my sound, almost giggling. Having begun to feel near alone in the bed I was thankful for at least this slight demonstration. Even if it was puzzling. Was she ridiculing my western way of verbalizing a joyous sex-blast? Or was she still thinking about the cat? I know I was.

I drew back onto all fours and rested my head on hers, trying not to breathe too heavily. Then I looked at her. Her smile was slightly beyond slight but her eyes were serious. It occurred to me that, where I was naked in the physical sense, this was just a state of merely being bare of clothing. But by Wei's conspicuous discernment, my nakedness of character was now a terrible exposure. Her expression transmitted concisely—stern brow, pursed lips—that I had not measured up. I rolled off.

Wei sighed.

I probed her lower region with limbered fingers, looking to work through to the end. She brushed me away.

"It okay."

"I want to."

"I not."

I ranged below, tongue at the ready.

"Stop!" She swatted me.

I lay back on the pillows with an arm folded behind my head.

Wei sighed again. "It okay." She took my willing hand in hers and met my eyes. "Nice."

We lay breathing. Silent minutes passed.

Kitty

Wei shifted and I knew she would be seeking her panties. Dressing. Leaving. This she did silently. Still faintly smiling as we kissed at the door.

I tried to read but couldn't concentrate, perhaps due to the residual Wei-scent in the bed. I turned off the light. Despite the post-sex calm I could not navigate a drift toward sleep, but entered a daydream.

The cat.

That morning.

Darting under my bed.

I snapped to. Could she still be under there? I turned the light back on.

This time I took a couple of breaths, planted my feet, and heaved with sufficient force to raise the bed high enough so I could fully inspect underneath. Although the light, as it reached to the far wall, was dim with the density of airborne dust, somewhere in the mustiness I noted movement. Then a pair of unmistakable spooky luminescent eyes. As my eyes adjusted I could see the cat coiled, mired in great grappling bunnies of hair-infused dust. She glared out from there with a riveting malevolence.

Cats are great at that, giving you a withering look. I admire them for it. She was flinging me a good one. A killer gaze of distilled feral malignancy. Gone was her earlier passive oblivion, her casual non-caring when she had been the awake one, the standing and alert one. Now there was a definite fire of betrayal in her pose. All this and she certainly wasn't moving.

"C'mon, kitty." I gestured with my head toward the window. "Get going, you crazy cat."

She just stared at me. Green eyes hardening dark toward blackness.

My arms were getting tired. I lowered the bed back down, finally sleepy. The kitty had looked about to rush off. I surmised it probably would once things were quiet. I drifted off, at least semi-convinced that things would resolve themselves in the night.

Morning came so soon that I had to bolt into the street like a desperado. I lucked onto a bus and was at the office just in time to overwork enough to compensate for being late.

That evening before dinner, Wei and I paused at my place to have a drink. I poured her a glass of Pinot blanc. She sat cross-legged on the futon watching me do a quick wardrobe change. At the restaurant, she got a call from her other job and we cabbed across town so I could see her off. She moonlighted at a busy sushi place, one of those cheap barns that makes its profit on volume. I admired her industry. She was made of tough stuff when it came to work. But I was more than a little miffed at the interruption. Plus, she was freely participating in one of the most ubiquitous North American culinary frauds: a Japanese restaurant staffed and run entirely by Chinese.

I went home steeped in ambivalence. Despite the resident doubt I had about any kind of legitimacy between Wei and me, I was nevertheless disappointed that the date had not ended in bed. At the same time I knew that such an outcome would have been another empty gesture—the rote performance of a tired funster's ritual—a tepid carnal process embarrassing in its pointlessness.

I showered, dived into the sack, and *New Yorker*-surfed for a solid two hours, hoping to lull myself to sleep. But after a stilted evening of fractured Wei communication and my splintered word structures, I still could not sleep for all the confusion, the mental rehash, the compulsive considering of things. I turned. Tossed. Developed a hard-on

Kitty

and ruminated it away. Eventually I settled on thoughts of the cat. That *felis catus*, that *Sylvestris* of my daydreams.

What about that *felis*, anyway? It had to be gone by now.

Thoughts of whiskers and fur made me wide-eyed. I worked at banishing the images. A yawn enveloped me and sleep approached.

But it was like being on the edge of urination—not knowing whether you could make it to the next town, through the whole movie, to the morning without getting up.

I knew I would be fighting myself all night if I didn't check things out, so I flung back the covers, flicked the bedside light on, and straightened to a standing position. Deep breath. I heaved the futon and frame and the down quilt and all the pillows so high that I could easily survey all that was below me.

"Kitty! What the hell are you still doing here?"

"Maw ..."

Impulsively I increased my lift and carefully leaned the whole bedworks over against the wall. Gently. So as not to harm the cat crouching livid among the fluff balls, her palpably hateful look undiminished from the night before.

But her glare did not affect me as much this time because in the one word she had spoken I had clearly heard a piteous note. A certain lack of lustre in her eyes spoke of fatigue and dehydration. I understood that it was a damn good thing I had checked on her and I would be doing her the greatest service in setting things finally right. I moved in slowly, noting with surprise that there was no odour of urine, no fecal nuggets, no disorder at all aside from a demarcated spot cleared amid the grunge. I touched her. She did not recoil. She let me get two hands on her and lift.

I walked us across the big empty room to the window, monitoring with pity the racy heartbeat in my fingers. I oddly kept thinking of Wei and me and how silly, silly, silly ... Then I was letting the cat go, setting her well across the sill so that she could easily duck under the window and out.

And indeed, once afoot she did not break pace but continued on her own. Having gone without water or food for two days and being confined in a space not larger than a shoe box and having endured overhead the creaks and rockings of human concourse, the kitty fled away stiff-tailed and did not look back to me even once, not even in a dream.

CLEAN OR DIRTY?

Lena hates to drive in the big city.

She barely tolerates the relative straight line to and from my place. Over the years, she has all but gone subliminal with the route in her head. She depends upon its unchanging intersections, lights, one-way streets, and parking opportunities for mental structure. Any deviation etches trouble-lines across her forehead.

Nevertheless, I drop the notion: "So. When you're heading out, I'll just catch a ride to the gym."

"Da-ad." She frowns. "I'm not going all the way over there."

"What? It's not that far off course."

"No."

"Okay ... Maybe just a lift for part of the way."

Lena's forehead de-wrinkles slightly, but despite the fact that she herself is a resident of a hectic city—albeit a smaller one than mine—and notwithstanding her fine motor skills and the splendid calibre of her car, I can see in her face and hear by the silence-enhanced ticking of the hall clock that the ban on my getting a lift remains.

But I cannot surrender: "Oh, for crying out loud. You can find your way easy."

"Dad. It's more complicated than that."

"Don't be silly."

"I don't want to get lost."

"You can't get lost. It's so simple. You just drop me off. Take a right. Another right. Go three blocks. Take a left and there you are."

"I'm already confused."

"Oh, okay. I'll just jump out at the corner. From there you turn right and go straight all the way and you don't have to turn again until you get to the freeway."

We sit at the breakfast table where we have just eaten her most oft-requested breakfast: rolled pancakes. She never misses an opportunity when visiting me or my mother to have them cooked for her. I cannot remember if I have ever explained to her my theory of the ancestral significance in her preference for them. They are a thicker kind of crêpe—I want to explain—a hearty, agrarian-class, sugar-bearing relative to the elegant French item you can buy on any street corner in Paris. They represent in flour and egg and butter the blunter genealogy of our Teutonic strain; the brooding tempers, obstinacy, husky physiques, and entrenched philosophies. It would be sweet, I think now—the morning of her departure from a holiday break, the last few minutes of a rare and precious togetherness—for us to be speaking of this. But I can tell by the quiet growing between us that the subject, for her, has turned more serious than food or heritage.

I speak to her as she stares ahead. "But you're such a good driver."

"I don't care. It's just so obnoxious around here."

"I thought you didn't mind it so much."

"Sometimes. But nowadays mostly I hate it."

"You hate it."

"It's so cold. It's too fast and ugly. It bugs me."

"Well. In that case I feel doubly honoured you're visiting me. But I hate to think you have to endure the urban terrors just to do that."

"Daddy, don't exaggerate. You're just bugging me more."

Clean or Dirty?

The thing is that we'd already had this conversation the evening before, strolling on our way to see a movie. Her words came as we stepped around a panhandler and girded our eardrums against the blare of an ambulance: "I hate this place!" She had to call it out, nearly attracting attention.

Nevertheless, I didn't quite hear her. "What? You hate this pace?"

"Hate this place."

"Hmm." The noise had died enough for us to speak in civil tones. "Define 'this place'."

"Here."

"Here ... here? You mean earth? British Columbia? Or do you mean figuratively? Your general phase of life? State of mind? Or just Granville and Broadway?"

"This city."

"Oh. Well. I don't know what to say to that. I mean. Look at this neighbourhood. The choicest bistros. Espresso joints. Live theatre. Bars with jazz playing in them. The west side's best two-dollar pizza slice. Cheap kitchen supplies. A big-box bookstore. A greasy-spoon that serves chow mein-flavoured burgers and burger-flavoured chow mein. What more could you want?"

"I don't know ..." She rolled her eyes and I knew I'd gone too far and too wild, naming off things I liked and she wasn't interested in. "It's just not home."

"Of course it isn't. Not yours. Not for more than twenty years. Not since you were one-and-a-half."

I certainly wished it felt at least a little like home to her. It is this yearning that weighs in my mind as we finish our crêpes. It is a thing of which we have scantly spoken down the visitation decades, through all the concentrated holiday celebrations, letters and calls and emails, and meticulously planned and executed summer fun-times. For me there would always be a permanent obligation—unstated but nonetheless mandatory—as real as the sugar and cinnamon left dusted upon our plates and the coffee puddles thickening at the bottoms of our cups. Thus I offer: "How is your mother?"

"Oh, fine."

"Rich and getting richer?"

"Well, she doesn't spend."

"Still acidic and nasty about anything out of the ordinary?"

"I'm trying to break her of it, but it's tough."

"Still afraid to go anywhere?"

"Yup."

"She gets it from her mother."

"I guess."

"And you get it from them."

"If you say so."

"I can remember. Your Nanny was a white-knuckler for anything but a bus. She could relax on a bus, especially those booze-runs down to Reno she and your Grampa used to take. They did so many, he got tired of the two-day-down, two-day-back thing and got her onto an airplane. It only happened once. Apparently she sat staring straight ahead and cutting off the circulation in the poor guy's arm. I picked them up at the airport. She was damn near catatonic."

"Well, she doesn't go anymore."

"There are casinos all over the place, nowadays."

"Yeah."

"Yeah."

Silence. I sigh within it. "Are you feeling okay about everything?"

"Daddy, that's a strange question."

"I'm sorry. But you seem almost kind of testy."

"It's still morning."

I look at a clock. Ten after eleven. "Oh, that's right …" Both Lena and her mother are notorious post-waking crab-heads. Although the hour is respectably close to noon, I know I am pushing the non-morning-person boundary.

We both sigh. I struggle to keep away from the sadness I still suffer over one year when she didn't show up for the holidays at all and even rebuffed all my attempts to speak to her via telephone or email or writing. Then my call from a season's repose in Europe—"Come to Venice. We can paddle around together"—to which she replied, "Why, are you lonely or something?" For years she projected disenchantment without explanation. It wasn't exactly school, she said when pressed, though a recent flagging of enthusiasm was vexing her. It wasn't relationships; she was a veteran by now. Work was fine but blah. It was just everything. Eventually she confessed to having sought psychiatric help. The spirit of our reassembly since my self-imposed exile overseas had materialized—if only thus—inside a laughing narration of how she had flushed her Prozac down the toilet. The one pill she had taken causing a dizzy head but also a lucidity of resolve to open her life back up to its available alternatives: revised plans for school, quitting her job, a new boyfriend.

"Is your stuff all packed?"

"Almost." Lena stands, plate in hand. "Does the dishwasher have dirty or clean?"

"Never mind. I'll get it later."

"Okay."

"I'll get my workout stuff."

Her sigh is audible.

As we bustle about there is too the detectable stoniness; her subtle, muffled bristling. I work through the fear in my scalp, collect my gym bag, and don the remedial exercise shoes designed to stave off an advancing case of pronation.

We trundle out to the sidewalk and stand before her metallic blue roadster parked perfectly before my townhouse door on the car-crowded street. We'd worked well together the day before: scouting the spot, me invigilating as a slow-packing family strapped in two toddlers and ponderously swung their minivan into traffic. Then standing pylon duty while Lena fetched the car—which we'd had to park blocks away—and steered it home amidst the desperate Saturday shopping and theatre parkers.

We pause at the curb. I note that we are both admiring the parking spot. Then we catch each other doing it and our mutual shamelessness becomes gravitational. We step close to each other, swinging our bags and smiling.

"Hey that was some teamwork, huh?"

"If you say so, Dad."

"What? You think getting a prime spot in front of my place is some kind of casual offering? Like it happens every day? Sweetheart, we can go weeks without a space here. And there we were stumbling on it simple as a prize at the bottom of a Cracker Jack box. Makes me almost want to be religious. It was positively provident."

Lena rolls her eyes and once again I know I've ventured too far from normalcy for her taste. She tenders her keychain and chirps the doors unlocked. I fight myself to remain silent at the outrage of creating needless noise in an already dinning cityscape. Besides, my admonitions to her have long been grudgingly recorded and always rebuffed.

Clean or Dirty?

We open our respective sides and load the back seat. The car is shiny and spotless. We take our seats. From my leather sinecure I admire the luminous curves from the undulant hood forward, down and away.

Lena starts the engine and lets it run. Her hand and arm seem independent, palming a caress over the gearshift and letting the emergency brake free in a deliberate, economical operation. Everything in her movements testifies to her attachment to this machine. Her eyes protectively scan the rear and side-view mirrors, gauging traffic. I calculate Lena's life in terms of her driving: She's owned this car for six years, one-quarter her total age. She has always been a responsible child—her mother parenting brilliantly to impart comportment and duty—thus her eagerness to get a driver's license while still a teen was not for a moment opposed by her parents.

We ooze out of the treasured spot. Lena calmly performs the left turn against speeding town-bound columns of SUVs and we cruise, her hands firmly upon the wheel. My mind is in neutral, taking the imperative to enjoy every motorized second, each expiring centimetre of transportation in the custody of my precious only child. I become conscious of the deep, cushioned seat beneath me. It is all-encompassing and warm. I avoid watching my darling drive because, in this kind of mood, I am known to get misty. Lena loathes it when I get misty. I do not wish to introduce distaste of any sort into this perfection of a moment.

But then, in only six blocks, it is over. Lena pulls her sleek auto snugly to the curb and we turn to each other.

"Bye, daughter."

"So long, father."

We giggle away our sarcasm and hug one-armed. Her use of "father" is exclusive to times when she needs me to remember that our life together is largely artifice—a function more of brunches, shopping, summer rentals, and freeway travel than lineage. I use "daughter" when I want to bring her as close as she was when she was an infant, despite our mutual knowledge that such sentiment is folly and has been ever since that day her mom backed a puffing Volkswagen down the driveway of a stifling suburban house and headed away; history, love, family, Lena in her child-seat—all going away.

I nearly choke at how little more time there is and plant a firm peck on her cheek. Then I grab my bag and get out.

She takes the corner like a pro—watching in all directions except mine—and in a second I am alone and walking. The only thing I am thankful for is the perfect timing of the walk-sign, which allows me to leave the scene directly. I am a wreck and glad to be striding along the sidewalk and sighting my objective three blocks farther on.

Walking thankfully increases blood circulation; I feel the opening of interior passageways, the creation of intrinsic warmth into some kind of emotional recovery. I quicken my pace and note immediately the tinctures of pain in my knees when I step too heavily. The twinges slightly deter me from thinking but in the end I must: There were the visits; much like this one. The payments; always made. The times one of us got sick and missed a turn; always forgiven. Long and reasonable conversations with her mother; fun enough, but touchy. The everyday morning of knowing each other; lost.

I ease back and let the scientific shoes pay out the strain through foot and ankle and tibia and femur and all the acute little connections behind the kneecaps. Still, once in a while there is a pang in my step, reminding me of the cost. I know I deserve this. For a second, a gasp closes my throat.

Clean or Dirty?

I let the walking do me good, breathing and swinging my arms. And I cannot put aside the fact that Lena has lived in a comfortable city all her life. Driven habitually her smug little car in its calm streams. Tooled about within an invincible familiarity.

When I reach the gym, I do not have dewy eyes. Things have been so amicable.

Part Three

Outcome

ROCKS, ICE, AND SNOW

Nick got home at the usual time. Two large men stood with their backs to him on the veranda; one of them—the biggest—was rapping on the door. Nick made a point of hitting the steps loud enough to make them turn around. This they did, like machines.

The less-big one smiled. "Are you Nick Douglas?"

"Uh-huh ..."

"Just the man we need to see."

At about ten feet out, Nick stopped and noted their haberdashery—suits, good ones but not ostentatious—and sensed by their expressions that they weren't going to say anything further until he said something. "Can I help you guys?"

"What luck." The one at the door was smiling while his eyes raked Nick up and down. "We could have missed you."

"What's up?"

"We're the police."

They watched him, he understood, for a reaction.

"Whew. That's a relief."

Both of them frowned. "How's that?"

"You could have been Jehovah's Witnesses."

It took the appropriate moment but Nick was rewarded with polite laughter.

The bigger one gestured. "Can we go up?"

"I don't know why not." Nick had meant to sound casual but a thickness in his throat rigidified the words as they took the air. The cops' expressions immediately gravened.

"Mr Douglas. We're here to ask you some questions regarding an investigation." Both had taken their hands out of their pockets. "We also have a warrant to search your residence."

This pushed some breath out of him. "Uh …"

The bigger one interrupted him. "Unless you're prepared …"

"Yeah?"

"Unless you're prepared to talk to us voluntarily."

"Well … Why wouldn't I?"

"If you do we might not have to toss your place."

"This isn't about that assault thing I witnessed at the bar last spring, is it? My friend Paul. I mean, I saw what happened but I thought all that got resolved …"

"Mr Douglas. We don't know what you're referring to."

"Oh. Well. Never mind."

"Are you gonna talk to us?"

"What about?"

"That we can tell you inside."

"Inside my house?"

"Uh-huh."

"Okay. Fine."

"Well good." The cops looked at each other, then back at him. "You're gonna co-operate."

"Would there be any other way?"

This got them smiling again and made it seem right for Nick to stick his briefcase under an arm, whip out keys, open the door, and lead them upstairs. They seemed grateful he'd taken the initiative and the sound of their single-file clomping behind him tended in an odd way to relieve tension. As he scampered to the top landing, though, Nick sensed that his nervous pace up the two flights might have alarmed the cops.

"Hey, hold up, there." The voice contained no humour.

Nick had a one-bedroom-plus-den at the top of a rickety former mansion on the east side. There was a large living room that he kept sparse, with the only three big chairs he owned in the middle of the floor. The best thing about the place was the kitchen, with its harbour-to-mountain panorama on two sides. The rent was low and occasionally not collected, the landlord being of a cocaine-addled, too-rich-for-his-own-good variety. Under an ice tray in the fridge there was a small amount of marijuana Nick's brother had left a year ago. Being a booze man, Nick had forgotten all about it. Remembering now, with cops in the house, made him at least slightly more nervous.

Nick unlocked the wide doors at the top of the landing and held them open for the two men. "My name's Dave." The least large of them held out a hand as they stood in the centre hallway. "This is Alan. We're detectives. Major crime section."

Nick shook hands.

Alan glanced around. "Can we sit ourselves down somewhere?"

"Well sure, but ... Shouldn't I ask you guys for identification?"

"Of course you can, but ..." Alan shrugged. "Don't we look like cops?"

"Well I guess you do but, ah ... for all I know you could still be JW's."

"Hah." Dave smiled widely and pulled a leather case from an inside pocket. "You have no idea why we would be talking to you today?" He flashed an official-looking disk of silver and gold.

"Other than that crazy bar fight thing, nope."

Alan huffed and moved toward the living room.

Nick took a careful look at Dave's credentials. "Thanks."

"Welcome. Shall we go keep my partner company?"

"Okay."

"Whoa!" Alan's voice carried easily. "You got a goddamn art gallery in here."

"Yes." Nick laid his briefcase on the coffee table. "An art gallery. That's the idea."

Dave replaced his badge and pulled out a notebook. "We hear you're a budding artist yourself."

"Hardly budding. I've been at it for twenty years." Nick gestured to the eight canvasses around the room. "These are mostly mine. I ..." He nearly missed the traded glances between the cops. "I didn't know the police department was so interested in local culture. You guys want to buy something?"

"Hah." Alan sauntered from the window and sat down.

Dave glanced to his notebook. "Mr Douglas, we have to ask you a few questions."

"You said that, yeah."

"Why don't we sit down?"

Nick and Dave took seats.

Dave turned to a page in his book and spoke without looking up. "Do you know a Mrs Madeline Beaumont?"

"Sure I do. She owns a gallery."

"Right. Is that all she does?"

"Well, she's pretty much the biggest adjudicator and sponsor and patron of everything that gets painted and shown and marketed in the whole city."

"Heh heh." Alan winked at his partner.

Nick shifted, uncomfortable. "What's going on here?"

"Mrs Beaumont filed a harassment complaint this morning. Know anything about that?"

"Harassment?"

"A death threat, actually. Took it pretty hard."

"I can imagine."

"Put her in the hospital."

"No way!"

"When did you see her last?" This from Alan, who had straightened his posture.

"I don't know, ah ... last week. There was an opening."

"The Cosmopolis Gallery."

"I guess that was the one."

"You guess?" Alan's tone rose a note.

"No no, I'm sure. It was Cosmopolis. I remember."

"Why did you say you guess?"

"It's just a figure of speech."

"Yeah, well ..." Alan leaned back and glanced askance. "That's the kind of business we're in."

"Huh?"

The two cops just looked at him.

Nick shook his head and threw up his hands. "Did my hearing just cut out?" He tried not to sound too incredulous but knew he was losing the struggle. "'The kind of business you're in'? 'Figures of speech'? If you don't mind my saying, that's some kind of wild *non sequitur* ..." His last sentence trailed off.

The cops stayed mute.

In the glare of their blank faces Nick soon found the pause

unbearable. "This is too weird …" He rolled his eyes. "Madeline being hassled? By whom? Why? And why come to me?"

"Look, ah … Mr Douglas." Dave paused and appeared to be choosing his words deliberately. "Nicholas. Maybe we've given you a bit of a start here …"

"A start! Hah."

"We can sometimes come on a little strong."

"Oh hell, don't hold back on my account."

"So let's throttle back here, shall we? Can we call you Nick?"

Nick shrugged. "You can call me Nick."

"Good." Dave wrote something in his notebook.

Alan tossed a nod toward the window he'd been standing at. "Issat your Karmann Ghia out there?"

"Uh-huh."

"Nice shape."

"Thanks."

"What year might it be?"

"Nineteen sixty-six."

"Damn near a collector's item."

"I suppose. I use it everyday, though. Its beauty is only skin deep, believe me. From the body down it's just an old beetle. Motor clicks like a sewing machine. Rust all over the place. They forgot to build in a defroster. In the rain you have to steer with one hand and squeegee with the other."

"Dependable, though."

"As only our German friends can ensure in a forty-year-old car that wasn't expensive in the first place."

"You mind telling us how you came by it?"

"Let's see. I bought it a hell of a long time ago from a guy named

Gus who drinks at the bar. He's a pal of Bill who's a pal of mine. I know Paul owned it at one point but didn't keep it because he's into British and American. European's more my style. I got it cheap, too. The bunch of them were living together and needed money for booze as I recall …"

"Whoa whoa. We don't need a whole genealogy. We're just trying to place your movements, okay?"

"My movements?"

"A car like yours is part of this thing we're investigating." Alan turned to Dave. "I think it was a much newer model, though."

Dave said nothing but sat jotting in his notebook.

Nick squirmed in his chair. "Would you guys please let me know what you need from me?"

"You do know Mrs Beaumont."

"Of course I know her, like I said. Every artist in town knows her."

"Artists." Alan sniffed.

"Yeah. Among other people, of course." Nick looked from one detective to the other and back. "You say somebody's bothering her?"

"Why else would we be here?" Alan now came on severe, it occurred to Nick, in a calculated way.

"Heh …" Nick managed a slackening of expression and the faintest chuckle. "Guess you guys have doubtless heard of the good-cop/bad-cop protocol …"

"Yeah, what of it?"

"Isn't that kind of stuff kind of trite by now?"

Alan stood up, plunged hands in pockets, and stared down at Nick. "Don't get smarmy with us."

Nick had a genuine moment of incredulity. "Smarmy! Heh heh …"

"What's your problem?"

"Smarmy!" Nick found that the giggles would not go away and regretted it.

"What's with you, fella?"

It was a moment before Nick could talk without chortling. "Don't you mean smart or wise-ass or impertinent or something? Or is 'smarmy' your special word for the day?"

"Think you're clever, huh?"

"Well ..." Nick still could not speak without a slight mirth. "I'll just have to leave that alone for now."

"For your information ..." Alan pointed violently at Dave, who had his pen poised above paper, observing. "My partner here, before he joined the cop-ranks, went to art school, you know."

"Uh-huh ..." Nick had conquered his giggles. "What does that have to do with anything?"

"Maybe Alan's getting off the track here." Dave gazed at his partner with a noticeable pall. "We should get on with this."

"I'd sure like it if you guys did."

"We have to know where you were today. And yesterday evening."

"When did this all happen?"

"That's not a question we can answer."

"Can answer, or will answer?"

"Smarmy." Alan's face darkened from where he leaned by the window. "Smarmy."

"Okay, okay." Nick decided to try to relax and mentally preserve this event for future inspiration or diversion or at least good cocktail party conversation. "I was where I am all the time. Last night I was at my studio and today I was at my job. After work I stopped at the bar for two beers and here I am."

"Your job is?"

"I'm an IT nerd at CheckOff Solutions Incorporated."

"What kind of place is that?"

"An employee accounts and general payroll subcontracting firm."

"You work with computers, *etcetera*?"

"All the time, *ad nausea*."

"One of those guys." Alan smirked, sitting back down. "And last night? You were at your studio?"

"Down on Pender Street. Near Granville."

"Anybody see you there?"

"Only about six dozen people. It's a co-op. We have a bunch of spaces on the second floor of an old warehouse. I say hi and bye to tons of people on the way in and the way out. I had coffee in the common room with a couple of friends, went with a crowd for drinks later on. Lots of people saw me."

Alan had waited for him to finish talking. "Why don't you paint in here?"

"It's a messy business." Nick waved a hand at the softwood floor. "I only hang my paintings here, I don't paint them here."

"These are yours?" Alan looked around anew.

"That's what I said, yeah."

Dave looked up from his scribbling. "They told us you were good."

"Who did?"

"The girls who work for Mrs Beaumont. They said it's a shame you never got a show in their gallery."

"You're kidding!"

"Why would we?"

"Man! That's amazing. I've been trying to get into the Bonsai Rooms for years." For some reason he couldn't stop himself grinning. "This is news to me."

"Funny news, it seems." Dave was watching him.

"Oh?"

"You're kind of yukking it up, there."

"I tend to chuckle a bit when I'm nervous."

"Well don't be nervous."

"I don't think I am. I'm more like ... hysterical, for want of a better term. I mean, what you're saying is unbelievable stuff to me."

"How so?"

"Oh man ... Where do I begin?"

"Just pick a place." Alan pitched in. "We're here to get a statement."

"Yeah?" Nick snapped to. "Should I get a lawyer?"

"Not necessarily."

"What does that mean?"

"It means ..." Dave clicked his pen and shifted in the chair, arms across knees. "It means we're just gathering background at this point."

Nick waited for more. Both cops were looking at him with some kind of expectation in their faces. Nick was getting used to this game and kept his mouth shut. Several uneasy seconds passed.

"Well ... you see, Mr Douglas." Dave finally spoke up. "Nick. We're at a preliminary stage."

He left the statement to hang, as—Nick now saw—was the custom.

"Well it can't be that preliminary. You don't go getting a search warrant for a guy's place unless there's something serious going on. And besides, I've always heard it's a good idea to get a lawyer when the cops talk to you."

"Look. Nick ..." Alan sounded genuinely concerned. "Now we've sat and talked awhile we see that you're a reasonable guy. Things are a little different. We wouldn't want to see you go to the expense of a lawyer just for nothing."

"Well. I appreciate that."

"Good." Dave smiled. "That's where we'd like to work from. Because maybe we can cover enough ground here so we won't have to come around and bother you again."

"I'd like that."

"We don't blame you." Dave went back to his notes. "But there is something we need to discuss. The fact of it is, and I hope you don't take this wrong, not everybody thinks you're a great artist."

"Oh yeah?"

"I'm sorry to put it to you that way."

"Don't worry about it, officer."

"Detective. Call me Dave."

"Well, Detective Dave, I'm a professional. I can take criticism. And to tell you the truth, sometimes I don't think I'm a good artist either."

"But you're good enough, aren't you?"

"Good enough for what?"

"Good enough in a given year to hang in any gallery in town. Good enough to be at Cosmopolis or the Bonsai or wherever."

"Probably. It's a matter of opinion, I guess."

"Well, our opinion is that you're good enough."

"Thanks. Huh. Maybe I've been wasting my time with openings and networking and publicists and all that. Maybe I should have just got the police department to promote me."

"Good. All right." Dave's unexpected grimace unsettled Nick in a strange way. "Let's get on with this."

"It's your show, Dave." Nick tried not to sound flip but knew he had.

"Okay, now we come to the important part. This is what we're here about, essentially." Dave paused. Nick was mystified as to what he seemed to want to convey. "Do you see what I mean?"

"No."

"It's what we've been talking about."

"My art?"

"Not exactly. More like the reason your art isn't more widely known."

Nick shook his head. "I'm not following."

"Our theory is that you haven't had as much exposure as you might have, had it not been for certain prejudices certain people harbour against you."

It took a moment for Nick to comprehend. "Certain people such as …" Though he deliberately let his words hang, the detectives seemed determined not to complete his sentence for him.

"… Mrs Beaumont." Dave finally obliged him.

"Right." Alan folded his arms across his chest and regarded Nick intently.

"Well. That is interesting. A motive. You have a theory about motive."

Dave seemed to ignore Nick's musings. "Do you know a guy named Kyle Grigson?"

"Absolutely. He writes for *Arts Weekly*."

"The entertainment paper."

"Right. He covers the gallery openings. Goes around taking pictures of people sweating into their Diors and Armanis. Does a real art-suck routine, if you ask me."

Both cops laughed.

"Glad you said it and not us." Alan was enjoying himself.

"So what about Kyle?"

"He says you have it in for Mrs Beaumont."

"Aw, for crying out loud! That's a myth. She has it in for me."

"We heard that too."

"And for no good reason."

"Oh, hold on there. Some people think there's a big reason. Apparently something called the bitch face incident?"

"What?"

"Bitch. Face. Incident." Alan seemed determined that Nick hear each word clearly.

"I'll be damned."

"That was what they called it."

"Who?"

"Mrs Beaumont's staff."

"Well whatever they want to call it, it was crap. Accidental. And Kyle should know, he helped it happen."

"So you do know about it."

"I've never heard it called the bitch slap incident, but …"

"Face. Bitch face."

"Or whatever. But I think I know now what you guys are talking about."

"Tell us about it."

"I don't know if I can, it's so stupid."

"Start from the beginning."

Nick strived to locate the best entry point for the tale but encountered only a vacuum. He looked from one of the granite-faced detectives to the other and nearly panicked for a moment, unable to talk.

"We haven't got all night, Nick."

"Oh, okay …" Nick's mouth was dry; he worked his jaw to create saliva. "First off … Thanks for asking me to relive just about the worst moment of my professional life."

"Nevertheless. We've heard a version of it from others, now we need to hear it from you."

"Oh man …" Nick hunched forward and rubbed his face with both hands, something he'd been wanting to do ever since coming home. It made him feel better but not better enough. "Well you know, for some reason Mrs Beaumont and I got off to a bad start ..." He straightened up in his chair. "We first met up about fifteen years ago. I was at Emily Carr, just about to graduate. One of my instructors took me for a celebratory lunch downtown and Madeline was sitting somewhere off with a bunch of other rich ladies. At that time she was thinking about opening a gallery and knew my teacher and we ended up sitting with them.

"My teacher introduced me as this next great sensation in the art world or something ridiculous like that and they all had a good bit of interest in me. So I yakked with all the ladies and Madeline was the friendliest of all."

"How friendly?" Dave's voice had a deadly flatness now.

Nick glared at him. "Nothing like that. She was ..." Nick glanced from man to man.

Both detectives eyed him.

"I mean, even then she was almost into her fifties. I was twenty-seven."

Alan tsked. "It's not impossible."

"Maybe not but it was this time. Over the years I've thought about it a lot. I mean, ironically, that was probably what she was looking for."

"But you weren't interested."

"Hell no. In fact, and this is another gaffe I'd like to reel back in if only I could turn back time, I actually paid more attention to one of her friends ..."

"Who was younger." Dave spoke with certainty.

"And prettier." Alan chimed in.

"Exactly." Nick sighed.

"The next time I saw her was a year or so later when she opened the

Bonsai. I went to the gala with a bunch of friends. I didn't actually get an invitation. In fact, even if her staff tried to invite me I'm not sure I had a viable address in those days. I was living illegally out of my studio. Most of us were. We crashed any event that came along for the free food and wine. Couldn't afford to miss that. And then there was the networking aspect. Some of my friends made out pretty good over time …"

"But not you."

"Nope." Nick eyed around his living room. "This is my only show right now."

"Why is that?"

"I'll tell you my theory. And it has to do with what we're talking about. So we're at this grand opening of the Bonsai Rooms and Madeline looks across the crowd at me like I'm an insect or something. She cups her mouth to the ear of one of her helpers and somebody comes over and tells me to leave.

"It was the only time before that or since that I've ever been kicked out of a place. Humiliating as hell. And none too good for my stature, if you look at it from that aspect. Reputation is everything in this business and I think mine was ruined that night. I've had some sales, sure, but not enough to make a living. I've had fans who thought I was hard done by. I mean, sure, I got invitations. Eventually a minor show at a community centre out in the burbs. But nothing to make a career. And here I am working a day job fifteen years later.

"By now most of the people I graduated with have either had major commissions or big jobs in teaching or at least a modest national reputation by way of a Canada Council grant or two. I'm still trying to get a show downtown. I've done all I could. I've sat on boards of directors of community arts councils, theatres, cultural publications, you name it. Every so often I'd run into Madeline, who by that time was a major force in the art scene all the way across the country. She was never more than barely civil to me.

"Then a couple of years ago I got lucky and made friends with this guy and his wife who wanted to open a gallery. They established Cosmopolis and wanted me for their inaugural showing, along with two other painters and a sculptor. It wasn't my own show but it was a major spot downtown and these people had a lot of money. It was my big break. I was on my way. Everything was great. They liked the canvasses I did. They had me supervise the hanging and the lights. I was rockin'.

"We had a healthy crowd for the pre-opening party. There was a band. Lots of noise. Kyle Grigson was there with his camera. He smirked at me across the room because he knew I had been sucking wind for so many years and for some reason he seems to think it's funny to see a guy struggle so much. He's a creepy a-hole and I'm not reluctant to pronounce on that. Wise-cracking sarcastic snob dickhead ..."

"We get you." Though Dave wound his pen in the air to indicate a wish to get on with the story his expression affirmed approval of the opinion Nick was conveying. "What happened then?"

"It was like out of a comedy script or something. We're in this big crush of bodies and Kyle gets close to me and starts yelling. The sound is total, people talking at the top of their vocal range. The band is honking out noise. The general hubbub ..."

"You don't exactly hear him." Dave was visibly hanging onto Nick's yarn.

"My ears aren't great at the best of times. I hurt them a lot working in a bottling plant during my student days. I can't hear well when there are loud sounds around, like in clubs. I can't carry on a conversation like some people seem to be able to.

"Anyway, Kyle points to another part of the room and barks something in my ear that sounds like: 'Sucky to see such a bitch face.' Or some such thing. Coming from him, I really thought that was what I heard. No matter how unlikely it was, I thought he was trying some kind of snide joke on me, as usual. He repeated it. I swear it still sounded just the same. I shrugged, pointed to my ears, tried to look as cool as I could in case he wanted to take my picture. Then I tried to ignore him. But he got all huffy and yelled it again. 'Sucky to see a bitch face.' I got worried that he might think I was pulling a Madeline Beaumont, snubbing him because of his hanger-on status or some such art-snob posturing manoeuvre or other. So then, because I was trying to be extra nice, I got close to him and yelled, 'Bitch face?' He said 'What?' I hollered again as hard as I could: 'Bitch face!'

"Then it happens." Alan spoke with a satisfied confidence. "Like in the worst movie you ever saw, the music stops just then."

"You know it." Nick sighed. "Suddenly it's all quiet. And Kyle isn't looking at me anymore, he's staring disgusted over my shoulder. And who the hell is standing right behind me within full earshot of my howling?"

Dave went back to writing. "Had you seen her come in?"

"Sure I had. She wouldn't have missed an event like that, even with me in it. By this time she wasn't just a gallery owner but also the commissioner of the city arts board, in charge of a hellish budget, in a position to help artists and venues and just about anybody else in the biz who might be trying to make a living. And after all these years I'm hoping she might give me an even break, maybe for my perseverance alone, maybe just for old times' sake.

"But the look on her face. I knew she'd heard me. I knew she'd likely been watching us across the floor. There was no way to explain it to her, joke it away or dismiss it offhand. The way she turned away and stomped off. I was puréed again, like instant breakfast. She stood glaring from the other side of the room. Kyle sputters and gawks at me and shouts, 'I said, funny to see you in this place.'

"I said, 'What?' My ears were ringing so bad I could barely hear myself talk. 'After all your work. I wanted to congratulate you,' Kyle says.

"Most of the crowd hadn't heard exactly what happened but I saw Madeline talking to the gallery people. When I got home there was a message on my answering machine. They were sorry, but they had to drop me out of the show. Something about funding not coming through at the last minute or something."

Nick had been leaning forward as he recounted his story, elbows on knees, his head mostly bowed. He looked up. "Do you guys mind if I have a drink?"

"It's your house, go right ahead."

He went to the hall, pulled scotch and a glass from the sideboard. "Anybody join me?"

"No thanks." The cops spoke in unison.

Nick poured, returned to his seat and sat down. He took a deep slug and sighed. "You know who I'd like to kill?" He let the statement hang until he sensed a new stiffness in the room.

Dave was staring at him. "We don't kid around about stuff like that."

With whisky beginning to warm him, Nick chose to simply gaze into nothingness.

A cell phone warbled. Alan fished it from inside his jacket. "Yeah?"

Dave narrowed eyes at his partner and motioned with his head to take the call elsewhere. The big detective lurched from his chair and strode to the hallway. Nick surmised that he ended up in the kitchen, where he could be heard grunting monosyllabically into the phone.

"We were expecting that call." Dave spoke quietly. "It might just clear things right up."

"Huh." Nick was barely listening, enjoying his drink and winding down. He made a promise to himself never to tell that story again under any circumstances.

Then Alan was back. He flumped into his chair and gestured at Nick with the cell phone, looking at Dave. "He said it was what time he was at this studio place last night?"

"He didn't say."

"From six to around eleven-thirty."

Alan turned to Nick. "You got witnesses?"

"I told you ..."

Dave stood up. "Come on." He touched his partner's arm and they strode out of the room. Nick could hear muffled conversation from his kitchen but did not try too hard to discern what was being said, feeling sure he would be duly apprised. The detectives were back with him in three minutes.

"Thanks a lot, Nick." Dave was putting away his pen. "We'll be running along now."

"Yeah." Alan pocketed his phone.

"That's it?"

"Yup. Case closed."

"But what about Madeline? Who's threatening her?"

"We're pretty sure now it's family-related."

"Oh yeah?"

"Sorry to take up your time." Dave nudged Nick on the arm. "This was just us being over-anal."

"Oh."

"And, uh ..." Dave drew a folded paper from an inside pocket. "We won't need this search warrant after all."

"Much appreciated."

Nick stood.

Dave peered closely at a canvas. "This is excellent. Honestly."

"Thanks."

"Especially this one." The detective went to a street scene Nick had done during what he called his 'urban-naturalist' period. "Great layers. Texture." He pointed. "I enjoy your treatment of stasis."

"So Alan wasn't kidding. You are an art-head."

"I was one semester short at Ryerson."

"Oh yeah?" Nick was feeling better. "What years?"

"Early eighties."

"I was there a little before that. Just for a year."

"Good school."

"Did you know Stewardson?"

"Stewardson was my advisor."

"No kidding!"

Dave surveyed the other paintings, strolling slow with hands behind his back. "Yeah I did nearly the whole biscuit."

"Oils? Watercolour?"

"And acrylics."

"Well ..." Nick swilled his drink, almost happy. "Why didn't you say so?"

"I'm a cop now."

"Well you know, ah ... All things considered, that makes more sense than it might look like at first. I mean, you know the theory. Painting brings the senses together with reason and mathematics in a scientific practice, blah blah blah."

"Yeah ..." Dave smiled. "But how do you reconcile bureaucracy, routine, squalor, and boredom with the notion of the inspired craftsman creating earthly beauty as a reflection of the absolute?"

"Hmm. Absolute cop-ism?"

"Speaking of which ..." Alan straightened from where with a meaty hand he had leaned on an armchair. "We gotta get going."

"Hold on a sec." Dave examined another painting. "Brush strokes kind of muddy."

"How is old Stewardson these days?"

"Haven't seen him in years. But he was fine, last I heard."

"I used to keep up with him, but when I came out west ..."

"Best history-in-art man I ever met."

"I'll say. You did his Group of Seven course?"

"You too, right?"

"Rocks, ice, and snow ..." Nick dredged his aesthetics memory. "Some timber but mostly burned ..."

"... Rough, splashy, meaningless, blatant plastering and massing of unpleasant colours in weird landscapes."

They stopped talking. Dave pointed to another of the street studies. "That's this place, isn't it?"

"Right"

"Looks like you've painted every leaf."

"But I didn't."

"No, you didn't. Brilliant."

They paused together. Nick's chest was beginning to swell and he knew it wasn't the liquor.

"Some stupid looking car ..." Alan had joined them at the canvas, pointing to a detail. "The Karmann Ghia."

"Alan!" Dave flung the word. "Will you keep your goddamn mouth shut for just one goddamn minute!"

Nick had to firm himself not to step backward.

Alan flexed as if shot, then recovered and grew an ugly sneer to banish whatever vulnerability he'd let briefly show. Without a word he stepped from the room and began a loud descent of the stairs. Dave sighed, straightened his tie, nodded Nick's way, then followed his partner.

Nick moved to the front window and watched as the tops of the cops' heads materialized below and glided down the veranda stairs, through the hedge and away. He felt good, standing in his home, in the room with his images all around. The big old house felt particularly good, though the neighbourhood had declined. The prostitutes had been hounded out of the West End and their transactional madhouse had popped up on these street corners. He didn't mind the condoms in the gutter, the cackled dialogue below the windows, even the bikers playing Frisbee out by his car. But the traffic noise made sleep a challenge. That was the worst part, trying to show up at a full-time job with little or no sleep. Still, there were good reasons to be living here. He kept staring, studying, not moving, though he desired more of the drink in his hand. Something about the attitude of the unmarked police vehicle on the street: its routine colour; the rhythmic sling of the detectives as they deked into their respective sides—by his perception they wore hats, though in reality they did not—and the chestnut tree, maturing into autumn with promises of tint, then dissolution.

ONE OF THE WINTERS

It was yet another stab at getting Paul to stop drinking.

"We were talking to him, trying to hide things in barely concealed double-*entendres* the entire time." Simon sat on my couch. "Jeannie and I are too close these days. He knows I'm a pothead. He can't stand her pretension. And he was half-cut by the time we started. The whole thing was a doomed project from the first. I mean, he's always had a thing for her."

"Man ..." I knew what to say. "You couldn't have been less successful than me and Bill and Nick the day he damn near got stomped to death by that psycho, Gus."

"Hardly."

"Did he go bolt upright and run out to his car?"

"Didn't get the chance."

"Go on."

"We browbeat him like a school kid, told him he was missing out on life. Pointed out his unfulfilled promise. Not to mention the chronic impaired driving. He seemed to listen. Jeannie talked about their relationship. Nearly cried. We did a thorough job. You should have seen us."

I could picture them sitting around Paul's place. The stereo playing something like Miles Davis or Frank Zappa or one of the Winter brothers. It being midday Sunday, I could see the tumbler full of vodka and grapefruit Paul would be drinking. How he would cradle it near his crotch, half-lying on the couch with his feet on the coffee table. I could also see how Jeannie might distract things, perched beside him, skirt hiked to where you couldn't ignore.

"I hope she didn't pre-empt things like she usually does."

"She did take over. Eventually."

"Oh?"

"It went like this. We finished talking and Paul said fine and then we excused ourselves as planned and left him alone in a dramatic, you-could-hear-an-emotional-pin-drop sort of way. Gave him a cell number if he needed us. I thought it was effective. We went downstairs to her place. I knew she lived in the same building but I didn't realize it was directly below his."

"It's even the same configuration."

"Spooky, eh?"

"Was his music loud?"

"No. But enough to hear."

"Did she make tea?"

"She tried. I don't think that woman can boil water."

"I got tea from her one time."

"Well." Simon stopped. "Did you know she studied *su-pap*?"

"What's that?"

"It's weird. It's like I said. She took over. She knows how to do it. I knew right away what she was doing, and the hook was, I once had this lascivious West Indian co-worker who explained it to me. He pronounced it with the accent like Bob Marley. At first I thought he was talking about food; soup-app."

"Which means?"

"Literally, in the patois, it's a mangling of the French adjective *superbe*, which generally means what it means in English; good,

One of the Winters

superlative, like that. In the sense he was using it, however, it refers oddly to the quality of a valve. For which the French word is *soupape*. Workmen refer to their plumbing jobs as *su-pap* when things are perfectly snug."

"This is quite an education."

"That's our Jeannie. She knew the term when I told it to her. I guess in Jamaica that one time …"

"I think I remember."

"Anyway. The other usage has to do with the reason some guys will throw it all away. Leave wife and family and destroy themselves for a so-called *su-pap* mistress. It's on the level of voodoo almost. *Su-pap.* It's mostly more experienced women, not too old but certainly not the beginners. And generally ones who would not have had children. She practices timing and develops the right muscle-tone in the right places and at the perfect moment she constricts."

"And it …?"

"Well it drives a guy … out of his mind. A wild blasting cumload. The crack cocaine of male orgasms. Jeannie knew all about this. The complete performance involves the meeting of eyes, chanting …"

"So …" I looked Simon up and down. "Jeannie, huh?"

"Yeah. I must admit. Despite her encroaching heft."

"There is that."

He sighed. "We could hear above us." Looked into his glass. "His moving around."

"I'm proud you didn't let that bother you."

"Naw."

"Were you quiet?"

"When she tightened, I tried."

"Were you quiet?"

Simon smiled. "Enough for Paul?"

"Were you quiet?"

"I hope so. I might not be sure."

"Well. He heard, then."

"Maybe."

"Remember, this guy hears a paperclip in his glovebox. A leaky tappet in a V8. He's heard the rustle of my grocery bags half a block away and met me at the door. Like an owl, this guy."

"Then he heard. For sure."

"Hmm. Bad judgment on your part."

"Granted."

"But …"

"But, but, but."

"Panties?"

"Panties!"

"Huh. Well. When it's there, it's there. Nobody resists panties when they hit the floor."

"And I grabbed it. Yeah."

"Good man. Although I'm not sure I'd have done the same, even aside from the venue, which couldn't have been more precarious. But I admit, you take panty where you get panty."

"Amen."

"I'm approaching an age where the complications bother me just enough."

"Me too, someday, I guess."

I drank more wine. "I'll tell you one good thing. Booze might at least be considered a final answer to the sex-vulnerability question. After the third glass, no matter how hot the situation, I'm not going to measure … into the breach. *Su-pap* or no *su-pap*."

"All the time, for sure?"

"The jury's still slightly out. I haven't told you about Jennica."

"Who's Jennica?"

"This short, sharp, nasty involvement during my last months at the old job."

"How young?"

"So young that she pronounces her name valley-girl. Something like Jenna-Ka with a question mark after it. Accent heavy on the second syllable. Sounded like a soft drink."

"I'm getting a hard-on."

"That's what I mean. Even half-soused I was ready-aye-ready. But we had an experience that imparted sudden and enduring flaccidity, and it evolved not just from booze but from violence too."

"Not sure where this is getting us in the present discussion, but let fly."

"She had peculiarities. You had to start out with latex all around. If there was such a thing as a full body condom she'd want you to wear one. As it was, I went through hundreds of dollars worth. Fair enough."

"Fair enough."

"But it was the rote aspect. She liked the full-on charge. Lots of linear bang action. I once tried to thrill her by fluttering around, tickling her in places she didn't get with the square drive. But she disabled me plenty quick on that. She wanted it on a narrow rut; straight in, straight out. A control thing, I later gathered, no surprises.

"So after the first blastoff of an average session—she was tight, it would only take a few minutes—for our second and third go-round I'd be ramming her relentless and straight as possible. But with a hot rubber on, she'd get dryish and this burning-tire smell would start to rise up. Fill the whole room. It would get to the point of discomfort and we'd have to quit. I'd go soft. The thing would ooze off.

"Then it got weird. She liked to get up after that and walk around and wave her bottom in front of me. I'd thus be encouraged to slam in bareback from behind with her leaning against a wall or over a table or wherever I caught her. We'd surge, her taking it like a paid professional. I'd blow standing up, easily finishing with all that latex gone. In her hallway or kitchen or wherever. Careful to pull out and spray to the side or downward, often onto our feet. I remember one splooge quite clearly. A full white pencil-line from the end of my stiff-staring truncheon all the unbroken way down to her ankle.

"She saw it too. And something about it made her angry. She never said why. She ended up peevish like a wet cat. The pattern tended to repeat. The arguments would start."

"About what?"

"Exactly."

"Uh-huh."

"So we broke up and got back together and broke up again and stopped seeing each other and then resumed back and forth a bunch of times in a relatively short time. Instability the rule."

"That's always a drag."

"But she could raise up these immense hard-ons ..."

"A terrible factor."

"Agreed. So, predictably, the night she finally did go full-on florid it was the bitter absolute end. Utter deterrence. I mean we've never seen each other since."

"An epic split."

"Grandiose. It's an amazing story."

"Which you will now tell."

"Most certainly." I drank the rest of my glass and leaned for the bottle. "We'd been apart for a few weeks. She asked if I'd had sex in the interim. Normally, of course, I would lie about a thing like that. But having lived, as you know, in deceit for so many years, I was sick of not being myself. In fact at that point I was damn proud to be at least a month clean and sober from all forms of untruth. It took a hell of an effort and I wasn't about to break the chain. So I handed her an honest answer.

"Her face was turned away at the precise moment, so I didn't see any contortions or anything. But I did sense something red rising up. Still. The first punch I thought was just joking. She didn't say anything. Started throwing combinations. I had to duck. Then she started using her feet.

"For some reason, though appalled, I'd been nearly premonitory about the thing. Prepared, so to speak. I cannot explain this, but I was. At the same time I understood that words were irrelevant. She was demonstrating this herself. Not a word spoken. Just pure action. Very male, by the way. It felt weird. So anyway, without a word, fending off blows, I carefully gathered my clothes, made for the hallway, picked up my shoes. All the while with her hailing punches down and kicking my lower body. I held my stuff with one arm and fended with the other. I got the apartment door open—it was about two in the morning so I knew I had a reasonable chance to be naked in the hallway with nobody knowing—and I knew she'd slam it loud behind me. So I damped it with one hand and an unprotected butt-cheek. It eased quietly shut."

"That was a nice touch. If you have to be thrown naked out of a woman's apartment in the middle of the night …"

"And we all do sooner or later."

"I suppose. Then at least make sure nobody gets woken up by it."

"Thanks for that. Anyway, ever since. I've been slowing down."

"Epiphany?"

"Maybe not all that way. But I had a moment, slipping my duds on in that cold hallway, not looking up for fear of seeing somebody seeing me. I had a moment. I understood right then with dead certainty that we're not going to be doing this forever."

"Of course not."

"I have to admit, though, I hadn't taken a full breath for, like, two minutes. My heart was going one-sixty. My mind was crystalline. My arms and legs were limber, the places she'd hit me positively glowing."

"In other words you …"

"Never felt more alive."

"Hah! The old combat-adrenaline syndrome."

"Whatever. I'm certainly glad it happened."

"You had yourself a memorable event."

"There's something about being pummelled by a nude woman."

"You don't have to be into anything even slightly odd to appreciate the tableau."

"That's exactly what it was. I turned back and caught a full picture of her just as she lunged at the door, her face a rage, her body hard and working. Feral. Timeless. A perfect human sculpture. I've got a feeling it might be the most profound moment of observation I ever have."

"Be glad it's there."

"Oh, it's there. Forever."

"Good man."

"Makes for terrific narrative, doesn't it?"

"Anger in motion always does."

We sat drinking.

"But more to the point, and this is what I essentially wanted to convey, all the reference manuals say it's best and most likely that you meet your true love through friends."

"From adventure to romance. Good segue, nicely done. That's what I like about you."

"I can't just tell you a lascivious one without filling you in on my more honorable exploits. It's what's firing my motor these days. It's the payoff, I like to think, for all this obnoxious honesty I'm trying to practice."

"You're talking about your new girl. Liza."

"I am."

"Well do tell. This might be even more instructive than your last anecdote."

"Quite possibly."

"Please proceed."

"I will but where was I? Oh yes. You meet the best people through friends. Well. That had never worked for me. But this time she was a friend of a friend you don't know who claimed we had met years before, though I could not remember. We stood talking at a party we might have both missed, oblivious to everybody else. All I knew for sure was my intoxication on first vision, our imperative to conversation, an irrepressible hand-to-waist kinesis, the sense that we were supposed to meet, and the complication of her marriage."

"Ouch."

"Yes indeed. When I heard about her status it threw me. I declined an invitation to go with her and some friends to a club, I preferred the solitude of the party to reflect on my interior clamour. Hours later there was a strategy meeting of the sober components of my mind. Days later I went to her shop at opening time and offered to get coffee. Several times this happened. We kissed outside a restaurant three weeks later and then it was months of us trying to avoid togetherness, her disentangling, me serving alone-time."

"I remember the period."

"It was un-fun. Especially since I still had residual girlfriends passing through who needed handling. But whatever, that's another story. And then she was mine."

"Lovely."

"Then the car fire happened."

"Whoa."

"She'd half-sold, half-loaned this decrepit Escort she was driving to her friend Triece—who you once met, I believe—and it spontaneously combusted outside a McDonald's in Chilliwack. The firefighters said they thought it started near the battery. Liza was aghast. She had loved that car and wanted it to go to a good home. And then there was the question of insurance, there being, of course, none. In her circle of artsy friends, incomes sparse if at all—most hold on with welfare and part-timing in fast food outlets—the extra few dozen dollars is dear. No one thinks of buying specified perils to cover fire and theft. Triece had taken the car on the agreement that she would slowly raise five hundred dollars and dribble it Liza's way. Now there was no car and she could not commute to her new job and fate was kicking people around and there was tension in the air where the money had gasified.

"So Liza and I went shopping. We rode a bus to the used car lots on the East Side, want-ad clippings in our pockets. It was the first major outing of our lives together and she was dressed in glorious Salvation Army chic: Strappy shoes, slinky mid-length skirt with cowgirls on it, sock-monkey T-shirt, brilliant-red overcoat, bright bandanna. A drunk along Hastings Street laughed our way and said, 'Hey pretty lady, what you doin' with the square?'

"And it was true. I looked like a Mormon beside her. She just laughed and we persevered, holding hands all the way. But eventually we had to give up. Lots and lots of sketchy vehicles, a few too many greasy salespeople, too many sit-downs in cheap offices, lists of costs with arbitrary sums, too much paint-over-rust.

"We wandered downtown for dinner at that Indian place on the inexpensive part of Robson. Tandoori cauliflower, rice, Kingfisher lager. I remember it all. Then a movie at Cinémathèque, part of a Czechoslovakian festival with somber faces and laughable subtitles. After that we strolled and heard tunes coming from the Marine Club. We paid the cover, drank three-dollar shots until last call, and danced.

"Liza told me she used to sing there. I told her something noble like 'You will sing here again, my dear.'

"It was two-thirty and we were taking a cab home. Liza sat close. She kissed my cheek and then she seemed to know to lift herself when I ran hands on her thighs and under the skirt and all the way up. She let me slip her panties all the way off and over her sweet little shoes and into a pocket of my tweed sports jacket. All this without a word spoken."

"Impressive."

"I'll say. It was later I realized we did it silent. That's when I knew we were going to last past next season, past inevitable routine, past disagreement and fuss, past crisis and pain, all the way to acceptance and comfort, subtle joy and the absence of want."

"Damn you can be poetic when you want to be."

"That's what it does to you, boy."

"Hmm."

"Yeah."

"And we realized we didn't need a car."

"Because of course you agreed to share the van."

"You have it precisely."

"Uh-huh."

We sat.

I remembered something. "Did you know it's rumoured Paul has the longest member anybody has ever seen?"

"Jeannie mentioned it several times."

"When?"

"During the intervention. It became a talking point. The waste of it all. Squandering of potential. Non-use of the hand fate deals you. A physical metaphor for his lack of follow-through."

"Hmmm ... Not sure metaphors are going to do the trick in this case."

"How about Jenna-Ka question mark? Would she knock some notice into him?"

We laughed.

"Maybe we can bribe Jeannie to bash him a few times."

Later on, we had drunk most of the bottle.

"What're we going to do?"

"You know how sensitive he is. We must be subtle. We don't want to kill him." I considered. "Who was it he had playing?"

"What? Music?"

"Yeah."

"Oh, all night it was Miles or Frank or one of the Winters."

"Which one, then?"

"One of the Winters."

ANTICIPATED RESULTS

One sluggish morning Rodney showed me a story about a terrible crime that had happened. By the redness of his eyes I could see that the nature of it threatened him down to the toenails.

"See." He tapped a knuckle at the newspaper on his desk. "It's like I told you."

I looked. "Yeah, I saw it. Husband Helpless During Wife's Brutal Assault."

"Can you believe it?"

"No, I can't. Just how the hell do you sweetly rape a person?"

"What?"

"It's this ridiculous newspaperese emotional over-hype that never seems to heal up. No matter how many letters to the editor or late night TV comedy routines they do. The headline writers and"—I picked up the paper to look closer—"the reporters alike. They all use this dumb brutal-this and vicious-that to express what is already as nasty a deal as nobody should ever have to endure." I put the paper back down. "I mean, can you gently murder someone? And would it ever get reported that way?"

"Well ... That's not my point."

"What is your point, Rod?"

He railed, peevish. "Don't be so impish, okay?"

"Why so serious?" I sniggered. "Stuff like this happens all the time."

"Exactly!"

He sat back looking at me. Moments went by. Rod's eyes remained reddish. He said nothing more.

I gave up waiting. "So?"

"So. You think that's the whole story?"

I shook my head. "That's enough of the story."

"Think." Rod sat up straight. "There's more to this. Imagine the situation."

I reached. Mentally. Reached down deep into my murky intuitions of him—the decades-old data-banks of his observed sensitivities—and tried to re-imagine the scenario of the newspaper story from Rod's mind.

He eyed me and the newspaper alternately.

"Ahh ..." I offered this as a way of getting Rod to talk again.

"You get what I'm saying?"

"No." I had to be honest. "No, Rod. I'm afraid I don't."

He aimed down at the paper with the finger-barrel of a pistolized fist. "Did you read it carefully?"

"Sure, this morning when I first saw it. Some guys home-invade in the middle of the night to rob the place. May or may not be gang-related."

"Yeah."

"Grab the husband ..."

"And then?"

"Abuse the wife. Maybe as a kind of afterthought. They didn't intend to but as things played out it seemed like the appropriate thing to do."

"Exactly."

"So?"

"Think about it. They could have done him too."

"Did they?"

"It might not come right out and say so."

"It might?"

"It doesn't. Not in as many words."

"But you think they might have?"

"They were holding him down."

"One guy."

"Yeah. One guy is holding him down."

"When you think of it, depending on the size of everybody concerned, no matter how slight a guy might be, that'd be a tricky thing, if another guy is raping the wife."

"That's my point."

"What? That it's tough to hold a guy down while somebody's raping his wife?"

"Well, they tied him up before they did it, didn't they?"

"I must have missed that." I picked up the paper again. "But one would assume some such anyway."

"Whatever. That's not my point."

"What is your point?"

"That if they did that to her, then they could just as easily have done it to him too."

"I suppose so. If it all happened like it says it did in the newspaper."

"The newspapers report what the police tell them. The police tell what they want us to know. They've only just started their investigation, and they haven't got anybody in custody. They only know what the victims told them, and if they know more … Maybe they don't want to start a public panic."

"So …?" I put down the paper.

"So." Rod stood up. "It could have happened."

After lunch we were in Rod's office. I was using a fingernail to unstick a scrap of corn chip from between two molars. Rod had gone out and got a different newspaper. "See. It says here they tied him down."

"Rod, would you let the stupid thing go?"

"It's not stupid."

"It is to obsess about it. Let it go."

"I'll see."

"And besides ... We have greater concerns at hand."

"What? The re-organization?"

"What else?"

"Not much we can do about it. I'd guess they've already figured out who goes where."

"Maybe things will improve around here."

Rod gave me his don't-be-so-naïve-I-feel-like-kicking-you look. "The preliminary indications are not good. Like, what about this new floating manager position?"

"Apply. I am. Everybody else is."

"I suppose."

"What have you got to lose?"

"What have I got to win? The job description is way loosey-goosey."

"That can be a good thing. Define it yourself. Get into it and invent yourself a dream job."

"You make it sound so positive. Never mind that they'll be taking one of us and making them a boss and then things will never be the same."

"Sheesh. You make it all sound so dark."

Rod pulled a pair of scissors from his desk drawer and began snipping at the newspaper.

"What are you doing?"

Anticipated Results

"Keeping a file."

"You're pretty serious about this."

Rod looked up. "What's more serious than having a couple of goons rape your wife in front of you?"

His voice had a deadness I had not previously heard. I couldn't tell whether it was because of the crime talk or the job talk. I watched his hands with the paper and scissors. In the instant he'd looked at me, he'd nicked his paper-holding hand.

"Watch it." I pointed.

Rod looked down. "Damn."

He put the finger in his mouth. I stood up, intent to get to my office and the supply of dental floss that was there.

A couple of days later, Rod seemed even more grim than usual. We'd just had takeout Japanese food—both of us opted for the teriyaki chicken special—and sat sipping tepid green tea. I pulled out the toothpicks I had carefully made sure to bring along and offered him one. He looked at me quizzically.

"Go ahead. You look like you've got something stuck in there." I gestured to his head and hoped he'd appreciate a feeble attempt at joking.

"Yeah." Rod soberly took a toothpick. "I've been thinking."

"About tooth decay?"

"Naw." He didn't laugh. "About that break-and-enter rape business . . ."

"Hey, I thought we put that one past us. You have to live your life."

"I talked it over with her."

"Jeez. I don't know if you should have done that."

"You're right there." He raised his eyebrows. "She got pretty upset."

"Women generally seem to keep cool as long as they think someone else around them is keeping cool. But if they see you've lost your nerve, they can freak. Especially if it's their husband who's not keeping their cool."

"I haven't lost my nerve." Rod leaned across the table. "I've come to a plan of action."

"Oh?"

"Consider the situation. Two drug-crazed guys in balaclavas are raping your woman."

"I try not to think about that kind of stuff."

"Just imagine." Rod spoke as if he had not heard me. Judging by his intensity I sensed he had not. "It's happening whether you like it or not. What's the only thing that's going to help you out?"

"Superman?"

"Be serious."

"A telephone speed-dialed to 9-1-1 and sitting ignored in the corner recording the whole thing?"

"You're on your own. Nobody's going to help you. At least not in time."

"It's a pretty dire situation."

"It's game over. Unless you've taken steps to prepare."

"What does that mean?"

"What do you think?"

I shrugged. "Martial arts?"

"Or some such." Rod unconsciously flexed the hand that was not encompassing his teacup.

Then I woke up. I reconsidered Rod's grave tone, watched his clenching hand, and understood. I fought the impulse to blink incredulously but smiled and leaned in close. "Let me get this straight

..." I lowered my voice as much as possible without going to a whisper. "Some kind of weapon?"

Rod smiled.

"A gun?"

Rod nodded.

We were quiet then for too long a moment. I did not know whether to be confounded or congratulatory. All I could think about was how awkward he was with scissors. I cravenly reached for a quip: "You're gonna get yourself a rod, Rod?"

He smiled along with me. "Gonna get myself a gat, Nat."

"Gonna pack some heat, Pete?"

"Buyin' me some steel, Neil."

I sighed deep. "It's good we can kid about this."

"Yeah, I guess. But it's about as far away from a kidding situation as you want to get."

"You seem different to me now."

Rod brightened and threw his hands up. "The minute you make up your mind, you feel different."

I paused a minute. Tried to imagine myself holding a pistol. "Better?"

"Much." He laid both fists in front of him on the table.

"But what about the statistics? The accidents. Wacko family members. Irate wives. The break-and-enter artists who find the thing and use it against you or somebody else."

"Statistics never made me feel as good as this baby does."

"You've already gone ahead and got it?"

"I went shopping. Found what I want. Filled out the forms for an FAC ..."

"FAC?"

"Firearms acquisition certificate."

"Oh."

"I paid the fees and signed up for the course. Now I wait."

"You went to a gun store and bought a gun."

"It's an involved process. But yes. I bought a gun."

"No offence, my man, but ..." I sat back. "You're not so good with your hands, are you? I've watched. You're the world's worst driver. You took five years to learn to type. You can't load a stapler. In fact, you're a man who shouldn't be left alone with sharp scissors."

Rod was still smiling. "Look." He held out the finger. "Healed right up."

"You know what I'm talking about."

"I'll be fine. I'm taking a course."

"Last week you tripped down a flight of stairs and you weren't even drunk."

"That could have happened to anybody."

"You flunked shop in high school."

"I did not. I got a pass instead of a letter grade. That's all."

"You're the only guy I know who's been found 100 percent at fault for a car accident."

"That was bogus. You were there."

"Yeah, I saw you open your door into traffic and get it sheared off. Now I'm worried about you getting something else sheared off."

Rod waved a hand. "There's a different standard of safety when it comes to guns."

"I should hope so."

"And even though I've only handled it in the store ... the feeling you get. It's like drugs."

"Eerie you should mention the word drugs in the same conversation as the word gun."

"Oh, don't get all ironic on me."

"Irony has a cute way of turning around and biting you in the ass—or should I say shooting you in the foot?—just like gun ownership. Or so I've been told."

"That's not funny."

"It is so."

"It's not that big a deal."

"It is between us. I always thought we'd be able to deal with life's little exigencies with our heads, not bullets."

"We always hoped that."

"Yeah."

"Maybe this is using your head."

"I heavily doubt it."

"But you're not absolutely sure."

"Of course not."

"Well, then."

"Well, then." I broke off my admonitory stare. "I just don't know."

Rod had not flinched. "Neither do I." He pushed back from the table. "That's why I got the damn thing."

At quitting time, Rod went to his car and took off toward the suburbs. I'd been to his house many times. I pictured him pulling into the double-wide driveway and electronically opening one of the bays and parking his Lexus where it belonged, amid the seldom-used golf equipment and the ride-'em lawn mower that his wife could operate far better than he does. Rod's wife had been a friend of our crowd for years before the relationship got joinable and for all the uncertainty they'd had before marriage things had settled down to what, for me, would be a near-stultifying degree of conventionality. I knew she would greet him with a smile and probably worry out loud about house maintenance or the heating bill or her job. They would drink wine and have dinner. They would watch TV and/or go for a walk around the neighbourhood in the dusk. They would set the house alarm, go to sleep in their sprawling bedroom and she would cuddle close to Rod, whatever the temperature in the room.

Driving the short distance to my apartment I imagined all this as easily as watching a movie because I knew what Rod was about and was oddly glad he had something valued enough to be anxious over. The one slightly irksome aspect in our friendship was the fact that down all the years he had only been to my place once. We'd gone to a play and got dinner on a night when he would have been alone at home anyway because she was on some conference or other. We had a couple of scotches and yakked like frat boys. He verbally appreciated my minimalist furnishings and extra-big TV. We left his car at the office and I put him on the subway so he would not risk a DWI charge going home. That had all happened before Liza and I got together. He had not seen her cluttered and cute touches to my life. I did not know when he ever would.

I cooked up some snapper and asparagus and went to bed reading *The New Yorker*. Liza and a pal had been downtown at a screening of the latest *Dogme* film. When she got home she slipped into bed and snuggled close, transfixed me with frozen feet.

Nowhere in these two scenarios could I picture a firearm.

Next day at the office I resisted the impulse to point my finger and fire an imaginary round through Rod's doorway when I passed by. I opted just to stop and look in on him. He was alternately bending low over a notebook and scrolling through thick script on his computer screen.

"What have you got there, gunslinger?"
Rod swivelled around. "Management manual."
"Oh. That."
"Why aren't you studying?"
"I did. All that argotic gunk. It goes through one synapse and out another."
He wagged his head. "Interviews are next week."
"Yeah."
Rod turned back to his studying. "So."
"So …"

Walking back to my office with a cup of coffee I realized that a little more gun conversation was what I had actually been looking for. More edgy talk. Maybe something to make me feel like things weren't so ominous. But there was an immense file on my computer screen titled *Administrative Technologies* that had to be read. It hulked in a corner of my mind like a comic book villain. I sat down and gave it my best, but my psyche kept interrupting with images of muzzle flashes, bucking foresights, sprung hammers, rifled chambers, expanding gases hurtling lead projectiles toward writhing targets.

I struggled to shake my mind clear, kept running for coffee late into the evening, concentration hopelessly refracted.

Rod and I shared our next lunch right after the interviews. I was feeling crappy.

"You haven't touched your salmon." He pointed his chopsticks.
"I'm going to order some *sake*. Join me?"
"At lunch?"
"Why not?"

"We never drink at lunch."

"I think I'm gonna start."

"I'd be asleep by two-thirty."

"Today, I don't give damn."

"Jeesh. They must have put you through a real grinder."

"Didn't they do the same to you?"

"It was tough, but I felt fine afterward."

"So you think you did well?"

"I don't know for sure. I guess. Didn't you?"

"Hell, I don't know." I flagged the waiter and ordered my drink.

Rod paused his eating. "You studied, didn't you?"

"Loads. It was familiar enough stuff. Common sense, a lot of it. But you never know. I mean. Some of the questions were kind of twisted. I'm sure there were some trick ones in there. Like the one about organizational initiatives ..."

"Anticipated results ..."

"You had to tell them how you'd classify objectives for setting up a research committee and digging up material and take the appropriate action, et cetera blah blah."

Rod picked up a swatch of fried spinach. "Anticipated results."

I watched him. "Why do you keep on saying anticipated results?"

"That was the *argotic*—as you put it—key phrase answer to that question."

"What? You mean I didn't have to go on and on about program analysis and resource allocation and all that kind of stuff?"

"Yeah, you had to do that too but you had to work in the phrase 'anticipated results' somewhere along the line or, as I understand it, almost the whole answer doesn't count."

I rolled my eyes and knew that the *teppan* on my plate would not be good enough to wash away the taste that was developing in my mouth. "What?"

"Didn't you read the preamble?"

"Which one?"

"If you read the preamble to that big book they just put out about revised methodology you'd have noticed it right there. It said that the spirit of contemporary management philosophy resides in the notion of acknowledged aims and reasoned means to an identified goal ..." Rod ate as he spoke. "And the common expression of goals and values depends on an agreed upon and practicable set of illustrative terms. Or some such. Anyway, the ironclad patented label to that particular abstraction is ..." He took a bite.

"Anticipated results."

"They practically can't even hear you talking unless you say those magic words."

"Jeez."

Rod's brow furrowed. "At least that's what I think is the deal."

"It sounds revoltingly credible to me. Especially the revolting part."

"I'm pretty sure that's the deal."

"So I might as well have been telling them a bedtime story."

"Oh, come on." Rod attacked his plate yet again. "You're a seasoned pro. I'm sure you covered fine."

My *sake* arrived. I drank some, but Rod was right; drinking at lunch tasted like trouble. It certainly didn't take my mind off the misery of being uncertain. We ate.

"I'll tell you what's for sure, though."

"What's that?"

"I'm getting to be a darn good shot."

"You don't say."

"It's a hell of a thing. An ox like me."

"Finally, you're willing to admit it."

"You're right." He gesticulated dangerously, chopsticks in hand. "I'm a threat with a three-hole punch. But the instructors are careful, careful people. And you study safety in a classroom for hours before you do any firing. So far, I wouldn't even consider touching the thing off the shooting range."

"But you're a regular Deadeye Dick when you're there, huh?"

"You bet."

"Well." I held up a thimble of rice wine and toasted him. "Here's to accuracy." I belted the drink and it tasted worse than ever.

A week went by and then at the quarterly staff conference the word came down: Rodney was the new boss-in-training. They sent him out of the room and handed us our turndown letters personally. I was not surprised or particularly disappointed. If it wasn't going to be me I was happy Rod had got it over the others.

I fell into step beside him after the meeting. "I suppose you think you're pretty special now."

"Actually, I was feeling pretty special to begin with." Rod smiled. Then strode away.

It was about a month later—after Rod had been to admin orientation—that there was real change. I passed by his office and watched him for a moment, poring over papers.

"Hey, Boss. How are you?"

He looked up. "What's that?"

"How the heck are ya, hotshot?"

"Fine." His expression did not change. "How're you?"

"Good."

Rod said nothing.

The verbal hiatus became instantly awkward. I said: "How's the wife?"

"She's fine."

"Good. Does she like being married to an important man?"

Rod smiled only faintly. "She feels ..."

"Corporate?"

He frowned. "No."

"Serene?"

"I suppose, but ..."

"Saintly?"

Rod's expression did not change.

I leaned casually inside the door and tried chuckling to grease the joke a little. Rod barely grinned before slacking back to impassivity. Then he pursed his lips in a funny way and I knew he was about to try to say something careful and considered.

He leaned back in his chair. "She feels clear."

"Oh yeah?"

Rod nodded, silent, looking at me.

"Clear, you say."

"Yes. She does. She has clarity." He paused. Lightly rocked in his chair. "And so do I."

"Oh." The word hung long enough to create awkwardness. I straightened from my tilt against the doorjamb. "That's great."

"Yes, it is."

He went back to his work.

Shuffling away, I knew I too had clarity now. More than I could remember.

QUALICUM BEACH

Don't get me wrong ... he was a good man.

I completely believe that.

With what I've seen of life, I came to know he was a good man indeed. But not all good men have happy lives, and even good people can't help letting bitterness sometimes infect the hearts of those close to them. It might even be impossible.

Whatever. Almost since I can remember, we got on each other's nerves. He and my mother met when they were in their early twenties. They waited four years to get married and then another year to have me, so it wasn't a situation of accidental indenturing or anything like that. It was before the birth control pill, so you had to have your wits about you. My dad had that. In spades, you might say. Mom says he was uneasy during the pregnancy but perked up after I was born. I can only remember my father when he was angry about something—and it was usually aimed at me. I don't remember him yelling at Mom. The other children came much later on, so for a time there was only me.

As I grew up and went to school I had to adjust to changes in venue because we moved around a lot. Dad kept getting laid off or changing jobs. Things were not so good, even though this was a time in western Canada when you could make out fine with minimal education because of all the resource jobs that we're famous for in this country. My dad never went back to school to see if he could get something better. I guess he felt obligated to provide for the family, no matter what, and he was a traditional type. Once you were of a certain age, as far as he was concerned, you worked, you didn't go to school.

During my twelve years of public education, we changed addresses something like eight times. I was always an outsider; got used to it. Schoolyard bullies had me in their sights. I dealt with it internally, never got as physical as I might have. I certainly never told my folks about it because I had utterly no confidence in their ability to handle it. No sophistication. I just got tough inside. My dad was struggling, and I didn't want to add to that. Neither one of us could do anything about our respective predicaments. It felt equal in some weird way, a thing we had in common. But generally I just had to deal all through childhood with my dad's angry ways. Although he wasn't a typical post-war work-beast who ruled his family with an iron fist, and there wasn't a lot of physical terror that I recall ... I mean, there was some, but nothing like what truly abused children go through.

If I had to identify any incident during my growing-up years that defined what may or may not have troubled me, it would have to be the infamous wiener stick incident of 1962. I was nine. We were living, for a couple of years, over on the Island, Qualicum Beach. Dad had a job with the railroad as a telegraphy clerk, and we actually lived right there in the train station. Qualicum was and still is a resort town—in those days, it was tiny, a population of maybe 700, but the number tripled during the summer. My best pal, Randy, was a son of the local cop. We did great outdoor stuff. It was summer, and we were planning to camp overnight in the woods of the gully a little ways down the tracks. Randy got the idea that we should customize our wiener-roasting sticks by straightening out wire coat hangers and making neat handles and hooks on the ends. We worked all day on them. I was amazed how cool you could make a piece of wire look if you had tools—bench vices, pliers, steel wool.

I was late getting home for supper. Mom and Dad had just started eating, and I could sense there was tension, whether it was between them or just peevishness at my being late. I noticed the redness in my dad's eyes, though, and it almost stopped me from showing them my treasure, my personal wiener-roasting holder, which I proudly presented to them at the table before I sat down. Dad gave out a nasty laugh and stood and grabbed the thing before I could react. He said something like, "You never heard of a sharpened twig?" then took both ends of the wire and wrapped the thing in a couple of tight turns around my neck. He did it so fast I was out of breath. I started crying before I could talk. I remember his eyes, I keep coming back to that in my memory. I'd seen him angry before, all the time. But there was something else in there this time. A meanness. An evil, though I hesitate to use the word.

But you have to understand the times. Ask anybody from that era about small-town life in the 1950s. Sterility. Boredom. Up to this point, I'd suffered the standard kid's tension and emotional repression. I was used to an austere landscape, lack of colour in almost all aspects. I mean, the fifties lasted until at least 1968 on Vancouver Island. We barely had television. I have a photograph from that era—Mom, Dad, and me in front of the station—taken by a trainman with a box camera. It's in black and white. I've got a striped shirt on and a soup-bowl haircut, I swear, just like Dennis the Menace. Mom and Dad are standing together. I'm a little off to the side. I remember Dad rearranging us just before the guy snapped the picture. He pushed me away, now I recall, so that I would be standing apart. From Mom.

That was what was up. As Dad was wrapping that wire around my neck, he was like a jealous man. For years, we'd been competing for Mom's attention.

Years later, I had some understanding of the wiener-stick incident. But on that particular night, I ran out of the house without saying anything. I didn't want Dad to see my sobbing. While he was hurting me, Mom just sat there looking distressed. I'm sure she didn't want Dad to do what he did, but she never contradicted him in anything. Not that he was overly controlling with her, but I guess there wasn't any such thing as time-outs in those days or mediation or whatever else it is that makes life more liveable these days. It just felt like I was living in a cultural desert and an emotional dust-bowl.

Anyway, to keep to the saga, without saying anything, I just ran out of there and down into the woods where Randy and I had earlier planned to spend the night. Randy was having dinner at his place, so I had time to sit in our campsite and cry to myself. I unwound the coat hanger from about my neck. I wasn't sure what to do with it. With no tools around to straighten the wire, it remained a crippled, nasty reminder of my situation. Flinging it into the bush helped me stop crying. I sat back down and just contemplated what had happened while the sun sank low. Mostly, I was seized up by anger. In the history of my uneasy life with Dad, this incident was unprecedented. I couldn't imagine going back home. When it got dark, I rolled myself in a groundsheet and huddled under a cedar bow.

Randy never did show up. Later on, I found out he had begun to sniffle during dinner, and his mother wouldn't let him out. I would have liked some food, though the hunger did not hurt greatly, compared to what had happened. I just didn't know if I would ever be ready to go home. I wondered if they'd come looking for me; I wouldn't have been hard to find. I was ambivalent about whether or not I wanted them to. So I just sat there and quivered, nearly oblivious to the woodsy sounds around me.

Then, as my anger cooled and it got dark, I became more than aware of the sounds. Birds flitting by. Bats. Strange rustles in the bush. It got spookier as the gloom intensified. I felt myself slipping over into fear, a new emotion that day, and I didn't like it. I pressed my knees into my chest and clenched my fists until they hurt. Then I found a strength in resentment, remembering what Dad had done to me, how the wire had burned as it was wound around my neck. The image conjured up a powerful animus in my chest, a palpable thing, and I wasn't scared anymore. In fact, I laughed out loud. When I think of it, I've seldom been scared since. Not in any kind of visceral sense, anyway.

So eventually, I faded into sleep and woke up when the midnight freight train rumbled through. I was used to it when I was in my bed, right above the tracks, but sleeping out there under the stars it woke me up and reminded me of where I was and what had happened. But I still wasn't scared. I woke again with the bird racket around five in the morning. Even though it was clear, not wet, I shivered and had to stamp around the camp to warm up. I was hungry as hell. The bushes in the gully had a few early blackberries. I spent part of the morning on those, then as the sun rose higher, I wandered farther away, down the tracks, past the point of familiarity, across a rural road, and down it for a ways. After a while, I spotted a house through the trees, a place I'd maybe driven past in Dad's car, but it looked different on foot. I noticed things about it, like the slightly open windows and the full milk bottle sitting on the porch. We still had dairy delivery in those days. I walked on a little further and found a culvert with a stream of cold water. I drank deep, dipped my head under, and shook the water off like a dog. It felt good. Then I decided I had to do something about that bottle of milk.

When I got to the house, it was maybe nine in the morning. I was almost surprised to see the bottle still there. The weather was warm enough for milk to spoil if it didn't get into a refrigerator. I watched the house for a good half-hour. There was nobody around. My stomach growled louder than I'd ever heard it. I wondered if I shouldn't just go home, but the burn of that coat hanger around my neck stung too much. Still, when I started across the lawn toward the porch I begged myself to peel off, run back home, and get Mom to make me something to eat. It was a weekday, I reasoned, and Dad would be in the office. I wouldn't have to deal with him, at least not right away.

When I stepped onto the porch, there was the creak of weathered boards under my feet. I froze, fearing someone in the house hearing me. But no. I went to the bottle and put my hand on it. Still no alarm, no stirring from inside at all. A whiff of breeze brushed my hair, and the skin on my back prickled. I lifted the bottle, knowing I was crossing now into a primal realm of human existence.

I was so frightened at that moment that I surprised myself by laughing. Aloud. I guess it was panic, a nervous reaction. But I was truly entertained by the comedy of my thoughts. Even as a child, I was hip to symbolic significance.

Part of the problem was that I'd been happy being a good kid. Aside from the usual childhood antics—exasperating my mother, peeving my father—I'd never grossly misbehaved. But now here I was running from a strange house with my ill-gotten gains. I was an outlaw now. I found a lair and sucked down the whole quart in minutes. As soon as I tasted the milk, the sustenance of it, I knew how right it had been for me to take a hand in my own survival. I felt no responsibility other than to myself. I have to say it was a terrific feeling.

In the afternoon, I sat in a tree and watched my mother walk around the camp and through the blackberry bushes looking for me. She called my name. I weighed the idea of surrender. The idea of returning to a state of boyhood was attractive, but now that my stomach wasn't growling I could think more clearly. I decided I liked my state of non-grace and the liberating notion that somebody else had sent me here, somebody else had alienated me from ethics and responsibility. A free agent I was, rambling and impulsive. It was one of the few times I ever felt cool.

I let Mom wander for a while, and then she was gone. I knew there would be others coming around, and I would have to move. I climbed down from the tree and meandered through the gully, ducking into the shrubs when the up-Island passenger train streaked by on the tracks above. I didn't want anybody seeing me. I was badgered by thoughts of the house where I'd stolen the milk. There was a detail there, an element I sensed was important if I could only settle enough in my mind and calculate. I gravitated back toward the place and crept to a vantage point. I looked carefully at the porch and the surrounding grounds. I saw what I had thought I had remembered, a scrap of paper caught in a clump of weeds by the walk. I loped over, grabbed the paper, and slipped back into the trees.

The note said what I'd expected: No milk today. The breeze had swept it off the porch, the milkman had delivered inadvertently, and now I knew for sure that the house was empty and might continue to be for a reasonable time yet. It was entirely feasible for the windows to be open a crack. It was warm weather. This was a small town where everybody knew each other. People would normally go to town

Qualicum Beach

and leave their houses unlocked all day. I sprinted over the grass and stepped onto the porch. The front door was locked. That meant the occupants were gone for at least the day, likely the night, too. Or maybe they'd been away all night and were returning today; there was no way to be sure. The possibilities scraped through my mind and bothered me. I stood still and listened hard. Up the road, a car was approaching. I leapt behind a hedge. The car drew close but did not slow. It continued down the road. In the quiet, I scoped out the side of the house, the ground-floor windows, the porch furniture. I figured it all out. I was surprised at how good it felt, once I saw my way.

I let the scene unwind in my mind a few times before I made the move. Then it was like I was machinery; dragging over the Cape Cod chair, jumping onto the sill, pulling myself through the window, swinging my feet onto the living-room carpet. The weird silent sensation inside—the contrast from outside to in, a new world velvety smooth and startlingly different for such a familiar-type place—nearly unnerved me. I hadn't expected to so completely lose the sound of the birds, the ruffling breeze through the dogwood leaves in the yard. It occurred to me that in less than twenty-four hours I'd become a creature of the forest. That made things even more exotic, even more intoxicating, to prowl about a stranger's civilized place.

The notion of stealing money never came into my mind. The silverware was just commonplace junk to me. The thing was, at the age of nine, outside of a bicycle and enough money for comic books, there wasn't much I was interested in. But I passed through the kitchen and the sight of the bread-box and the humming refrigerator got my blood going. I fixed up a couple of peanut butter-and-jam sandwiches and went back through the house, unlocked the door, and sat on the porch swing, enjoying my food. I started to relax, so jazzed at solving my hunger problem that I forgot all else. I even stopped tensing whenever a car ambled down the road.

The peace of the summer afternoon, sun coming through the trees, the whisper of the breeze, my full tummy, the comfort of the cushions on the porch swing—these all conspired to make me sleepy. When I woke up there was a big '48 Mercury pulling onto the gravel drive. From where I sat, the grille and driver's side front wheel were visible. I heard a car door open and the sound of a foot crunching the ground. I lurched, groggy, stumbled off the porch, and bolted for the woods. I got most of the way across the lawn before the voice caught me, a man's. It popped like gunfire: "Boy!" It froze me like I was a mime, right there on the grass.

Why did I stop? Again, it was the times. If you were a kid in the fifties, you listened to adults. All adults. No questions asked. It was a pedophile's dream, those times; thank goodness that's more or less over. But it was a culture of strictness. The order of the era was obedience and conformity. There was no debate over adult priority. They were first and children followed; this was the universally accepted doctrine. You were an instant bastard to go against the crowd. You got punished. The other kids would ostracize you. It was like living inside a black-and-white movie.

Anyway, this man yelled "Boy!"—and I immediately stopped running. The guy didn't say anything more. I turned slowly around. He was probably middle-aged—all adults looked around forty-five years old in those days—dressed in a dark suit, with a red tie and a brown fedora. He was holding a cigarette between two fingers, the thumb covering the filter and manipulating the hot end downward, casual to the point of contempt. I especially remember the cigarette because my dad smoked and I absolutely loathed the smell of the damned things. Even then. In fact, Dad used to sit in the bathroom smoking and reading the newspaper, stinking away. To this day, I associate cigarettes with the smell of shit. And now that exact reeky pong swept at me on the breeze across the lawn of this man's house, and he just stood there, looking at me, fingering his smoke, the sunlight on him flickering through the trees, his elbow resting in the open window of the car, one foot resting on the running board.

The car was olive-green, one of those immense, curved, art-deco beauties they used to drive. I still think of those automobiles as rolling *objets d'art*. The beauty of it almost took me out of the scene, out of my terror, the image of that car in the soft evening light. But I had to look at the man's face eventually, and I saw a malevolence I had not expected. I'm sure he could see his front door left ajar and maybe even the jam still on my face. I looked guilty as hell.

But I was just a kid! This guy didn't know the whole story. He didn't know I'd had wire wrapped around my neck. Shouldn't he have understood that maybe something had happened to make me do what I had done? I was near frantic with indignation.

But the way he looked at me, full of assumption, full of bile—it was the most bogus prejudice I had ever experienced, and it still burns me. As if I was some kind of willing criminal. I've never forgotten. The injustice of it became the start of my darkness, the portal to a black will inside my soul. In that moment, I knew for the rest of my life I would never lack for badness.

So ...

There's not much else to tell. Just me and a strange man staring at each other on the back lawn of an old house in the woods forty-odd years ago. After about twenty seconds, I turned and ran. He never moved. I just ran away. I never saw him again.

There was no stretch in juvie. No probation or community service. There's never been any resolution to it.

In those days, they sent you to reform school. When I was a social worker, most of my caseload had had a sojourn in at least one of them. Even though it was only a bottle of milk and a peanut butter sandwich, I feared that something fatal like that could happen to me. I was glad to lope through the woods to the railroad tracks and make a bee-line for home. I never slowed below a trot until I ran right through the doorway of our living room.

Mom was cleaning up after dinner and Dad was out, I figured, at a volunteer fire department practice. When she saw me, Mom's face lost some tension and her hands unclenched the dishtowel she was using to wipe a plate. But she didn't hug me. She didn't say she was glad I was home. She only said: "Your father's been laid off." I stammered for something to say. I spurted out the only thing that came to mind under the circumstances: "I don't care."

Mom put down the plate and sat me at the kitchen table. "I know he was cruel to you," she said. I can't remember if I responded. I can't remember much of the conversation at all. I was still transfixed by the expression on that man's face, the guy I had left standing by his car in the driveway of the house I had broke-and-entered and stolen from. I fretted for a second that he might have followed me, or might know who I was and was driving over at that very moment. In any case, Mom and I had a little talk and she made me some supper, and then I had a bath and went to bed.

A few weeks later, we moved away. Dad got a job in a mill on the west coast. He and I never spoke about the incident, my running away. If the guy I stole the milk from ever reported anything, I never heard about it.

But Dad and I were, of course, more trenchantly estranged than ever. He worked and I went to school. That was it. And from the day of the coat-hanger incident forward, we stopped doing things together. Dad might have tried—I remember him trying to get me to talk, to get me going with him on something. But I resisted every move. I hardened into a gangster whenever he got near. We never went camping, didn't even speak of it. To this day I loathe the outdoors. In my teens, Dad wanted me to work in the mill, some lumber plant he was in at the time. I didn't listen. I think I never listened to him again. I've essentially never listened to anybody ever since.

In high school, I got into studying. Against his wishes I went to college, took philosophy, history, psych. I loved English. It bugged him. He considered illegitimate anything that did not involve the cutting of trees and/or the digging of minerals. It was your standard working-class versus academia thing. The stupid thing is, I wasn't actually an academic. I was just studying and doing things extra-enthusiastically at school because it pissed him off. He especially didn't like it when I left home to study. Didn't support that plan at all. Acted like it was some kind of betrayal against him, a rejection of his way of life. And in the meantime, he kept on drifting between various jobs. He was a hard luck case all the way down the line, what can I say? He fell down as a family man, despite having more kids. In his last ten years he charged full-on into derision, bitterness, and alcohol.

He eventually died without us getting anywhere. I've been a grieving wretch ever since. I never got a chance to tell him what I'd learned, what I'd reconsidered. I would have told him something like, "Dad, I'm glad you never got to see how I turned out, mainly because I happen not to be especially proud of everything that's happened, but I hope you understand now about your own responsibility in the thing.

I know you are capable of understanding, you at least taught me to be inquisitive, to read and learn, and I'm thankful to you for that. So I know you are sensitive, and I know you are an open wound to family feelings; your inexplicable sense of bitterness toward me, your general disappointment, which I can understand.

"The world, we have learned, can be a cold place, particularly for proud and opinionated independents like you and me. Many of the things I rail against these days in the world generally are translatable to the problems you had over the years with your vocational disappointments. I watched you throughout those years, and it did not do my heart any good to see you suffer and grow bitter. It hurt me deeply, I never told you, but it did. As dumb as that might have been, maybe it would have been a balm for you in those years when you seemed to think your life was a big nothing.

"But your life was certainly not a big nothing. The world should know that you and people like you had a hard go, dug in, and made it out, didn't have much left to understand the world you helped make, and got overrun by all the weird stuff that happened. You seemed to have problems; I couldn't help with that. I didn't know what I could help with. You were resistant to me before I ever got resistant to you. You seemed to regard me as an aberration, a monster you neither intended to create nor understood once you did.

"That being the case, I lost legitimacy in our family on matters that I might have had an interest in, particularly those concerning your own behaviour, which was shameful for many years. You were responsible for much pain and unhappiness for Mom and me and the others. You refused to enjoy yourself in our presence; you seemed intent on making sure no one could ever relax. You made demands that could never be met. You were abusive to me, ignored Mom, and grossly misunderstood our feelings. You whined and stagnated and self-inflicted your own depression, developed alcoholism and anger-tyranny as weapons against harmony for us. When your methods succeeded, you sat back and blamed us for the mess.

"I haven't even begun to talk about how I feel about Mom's disappointment and the heartsickness that imposes on me. She had such spirit, such yearning to break out of the boring cycle of her life with you. She wanted to be paid off for all the sacrifices, the years of self-denial. But what did she get? Misery. Alone in the house with you during the alcohol-psycho epoch of your last decade.

"I wish you'd have found a way to buck up, get momentum, quit your moping. Maybe you could have at least died trying to be a new man, or at least let the good person you were re-emerge and remind us of the lovely years when you were young and maybe didn't know how harsh things could get. Taken the experience and filed it, ran until you dropped, and then gotten up and grown out of your self-indulgent funk. Been a real person, stretched, and taken deep breaths. Looked to yourself for satisfaction rather than putting it on other people, especially us. Figured out what you wanted to do and then done it."

At least, I tell him that in my mind, when I'm trying to figure out how to handle myself.

But I never got a chance to lay all that stuff on him personally. He grew a tumour in his stomach the year I went away. They were in Campbell River by that time, a four-hour drive from school. I took time away as much as I could, but he faded fast. Then he was dead. But besides frustration at not having been able to talk to him more, I didn't feel much. I was sorry for Mom, mostly. In my heart, I was almost proud of myself for holding up. I was glad to be hard. The real emotions hit two years later when Mom got sick. I took a year off because the kids weren't quite old enough to care for themselves and I wanted to spend as much time with Mom as I could. I got to know her the best I've ever got to know anybody. She thrilled me with her courage, fading away and yet being strong for me, being up, even being funny. She tried to apologize for Dad, and she nearly succeeded. Then one long night in the hospital, she died, and I could see, in her final hours, how much she missed him and could only remember his goodness and how she grieved the loss of his utter love for her. I saw the relief she embraced when she slipped away, going to him. It made me feel so alone, even with my little sister and brothers there, I felt like I was evaporating. I could have dried up and turned to dust right on the spot.

I walked out of the hospital doomed. I had lost everything, and I hadn't seen it coming. Ever since, I've been trying to replace what I think I lost, what I think I missed out on, and I've only been successful in hurting a lot of people. Women especially, they're my specialty. I'm practically useless at anything else. The worst part of it is that when my mom died, I began to miss my father, really miss him in all respects. I regretted that I had mostly repressed memories of him, good and bad. I realized far too late that I had wanted him to keep living. Through my studies and school and navel-gazing, I had begun to understand things and thought I could help him. We could have grown up together.

ANGER

During a cold winter some years ago I went to Europe, ducking life. After a couple of weeks, I invited my daughter to see me.
 Her answer: "What's the matter, lonely over there?"

Home again, I went to the skin specialist appointment I'd tried to make before I'd left (I hadn't counted on the doctor's three-month waiting list). As a long-time eczema sufferer, I felt half-entitled to preferential treatment but never got it. So, better late than excessively late, here I was, half a year later.
 The doctor looked once around my bare body—his eyes raking my neck and back, legs, feet, and belly—then stopped, grim, at my chest. He pointed to a spread-out brown spot below my throat. "When did you notice this?"
 "Uh. I don't think I did notice it …"
 The thing lay at the nadir of the shirt-moulded "V," an area scorched bold by fifty years' sunlight. It was at the place where my friend Paul had warned me not to carry a pen—clasped in the folds just above the topmost-buttoned button—because of its threatening potential as a collector of microwaves, warping the cellular structures beneath, inducing mutation and causing trouble generally.

I had lunch with a new friend, a woman I'd been introduced to by a mutual acquaintance. She was worldly, tired, formerly ravishing. An expert at relationships, she claimed, having had so many. I instantly liked her. We yakked extensively and of course eventually got around to appraising our children: her two and my one. I mentioned my daughter's incuriosity. "It's worrisome. At least to me."

"Oh?"

"I mean, she's never been anywhere. I wrote her from Europe and offered her a ticket to come hang out. She scoffed at it."

"Scoffed?"

"Said something like, 'Getting lonely over there?'"

My friend stiffened. "I don't like to speculate, especially because I don't know you that well ..."

The skin doctor peered more closely at the spot. "Can you give me an idea how long it's been like this?"

"Well, it started as a mole, if I'm not mistaken. Then it sort of morphed into that spread-out brownish smear that it is right now. It hasn't been like that for long. It's not black, so I didn't give it much mind."

He drew an instrument from a drawer—a kind of scope, I could see—then flicked a switch and began scanning my chest with a coloured ray.

"...'Lonely'."

"Yeah, that's what she said. In a tough-like way, too. Curt. Testy. It surprised me, I have to say. Because we've had a pretty good relationship overall. No big issues other than my numerous marital rearrangements. She seems to have gotten used to them."

"I would say this may not be incuriosity, as you fear." My friend

Anger

paused, respectful, and, I could see, hesitant. "I think she's angry."
As she spoke I received the knowledge ...

"Humpf. I don't like it." My skin doctor is South African so this came out something like, "I doan (rhymes with bone) lie-kit."
"You don't, huh?" I knew before I was finished speaking that my words were superfluous, routine to the doctor; the typical response of a patient on the cusp of receiving important information, whose mental/emotional state defaulted to an overdeveloped ability to cover any dicey situation in a blanket of words.
"Basal cell carcinoma." His pronouncement was perfectly timed to shut me up.
"What's that?"
"What you have here, I suspect." He touched my chest with his scope. The cool of the metal felt strangely reassuring.

"Anger. Yes, that would be consistent. Her mother and I split when she was sixteen months old."
"That may not necessarily have done it."
"Maybe not, but I've been expecting retribution ever since."

"Lie back." The skin man gently guided me to prostration upon the paper-covered examination table.
"What might have caused it?"
"Many things. Heredity, injury, the sun ..." His words trailed as action took over. With nearly alarming deftness he pulled open a drawer, thwacked on a pair of latex gloves and was flicking at a syringe. Before any more conversation could occur the pin was in me, gently worked into the epidermis above my solar-tattooed sternum and feeding

anaesthetic to the area of interest. The scalpel was brandished before I thought to expect it, glinting by the scarce light of the closed-slat blinds cloaking the one window of the tiny room.

"Retribution?" She put down her fork and looked at me. "Hoo-boy, you do have a back-story, don't you?"

"Is it that easy to see?"

"You carry it in your face. I hope you don't mind my being so blunt. It's not polite to go around telling people such things. I used to do it a lot. I thought it was a boldness of character and a valiant expression of uncompromised honesty." She stopped talking, then seemed discomfited by the silence. "But I don't do it so much now."

"You can tell me anything you want."

"Think you can take it?"

"I hope so. If I can't that'll indicate something more than if I can, no?"

"Umm ..." She wrinkled her brow. "I think that makes some kind of sense."

"Sorry to be so obscure."

"I think I know what you were trying to say."

"I'll try to simplify. For some reason I can take rejection from my daughter. I don't like it, but I can take it." Saying the words made me gasp slightly. I hoped it wasn't visible. "Is that a good thing?"

"Of course not."

The doctor's narrowed eyes and set mouth revealed all the instruction I needed: a warrant to shut my trap, while, with precision and an odd gameness—an article I'd read about surgeons' cutting obsession came briefly to mind—he carved two neat crescents into my chest. I did not watch, but the silence in the room while my skin and tissue were dissected nearly unnerved me. Then with a culinary-style flick and careful lifting of the blade, my surgeon finished his work and I felt instantly free.

"What do you mean, of course not? Am I doing something bad by maintaining a dignified stoicism?"

She kneaded her temples with both hands. "I'm thinking, I'm thinking."

The doctor turned away, placing his instruments to the side, and returned with a thick, serious-looking bandage already unfurled and ready to paste. "Leave this on for two days." He firmly set the patch where it needed to be.

I lay staring at the ceiling while he washed his hands. It came thundering home to me that I had just been through a diagnosis of cancer, a case conference, prep for an operation, the actual operation, post-op care, and imminent discharge. All in a matter of about ninety seconds.

"You can dress."

I sat up.

The doctor leaned against his handy bureau of medical instrument-bearing drawers, for all the world an operating room sideboard, and regarded me. "Stay out of the sun."

"I always wear a hat. I'll try to get used to that sun block goop on my nose. I'll take vitamin D. From now on, it's T-shirts instead of button-ups."

"I've forgotten for the moment, and your chart is in the other room ..." He visibly relaxed with arms folded across his chest. "Is there a history of cancer in the family?"

"Not much. Everybody dies of heart disease before anything else gets a chance at them."

"I'll send this to the lab." He gestured to a petri dish on the counter and did not acknowledge my attempt at levity.

"Oh ..." I pulled on my pants. "Can I see it?"

"Anger is acidic."

"That's what you've been thinking about?"

"That's what I think is important to you. Right now. Regarding this thing with your daughter."

"Anger."

"Yes."

"Hers or mine?"

She only smiled at this.

It was a coin of me, lying presentable in its scientific environment. Slightly smaller than a dime. Pink-bordered.

The doctor dispassionately surveyed the sample. We both looked at it. The silence became ponderous. I required something medical to be said.

"So what was this called?"

"Basal cell. I'm quite sure but the lab will confirm it."

"How long will that take?"

"Usually about a fortnight."

"Oh ..."

"Two weeks."

"Of course." I gagged slightly at the doctor's misinterpretation. I hadn't been trying to translate South Africa-speak: I knew how much time a fortnight was. No, I was simply taken aback at the relative eternity this part of the procedure would take in comparison to that which had preceded it.

"I'll give you a call."

"Okay." I knew that here I must ask a question but struggled for content. "Uh ... is this a serious thing?"
"Certainly."
"Basal cell ...?"
"Carcinoma."
"It sure sounds serious."
"In the pantheon of cancers it is low on the scale for mortality. But if left untreated you do run a risk of localized necrosis."
"Whoa. That sounds even worse."
He nudged the dish with a knuckle. "This looks early. That's good."
"Glad to hear it."
"You will have a scar."
"To prove it." I smiled but he did not.
We were both looking at the biopsy sample again.
Desperate for more instant info, I said: "Nasty little thing ..."
The doctor turned away.

"What can I do about this?"
"Talk."
"Talk?"
"With her."
"I guessed that. Seriously, too, I suppose. It'll take some considering, I don't want to blow it. I may only get one chance. I suppose I should be prudent? Diplomatic?"
"What's your daughter like? Does she have trouble with full-on confrontation?"
"Hmm ... yeah."
"Oh."
"She's ..." I had to calculate. "Twenty-two. But she still uses the old hands-over-the-ears, I'm-not-listening childhood trick whenever I

want to discuss something heavy. It's like a private joke between us."

"So you joke around."

"Sure. It's the best part of our relationship."

"Well then, at least there's hope."

"You could say that about anything, though."

"I suppose ..."

Things went slack then, over the coffee.

She picked at her dessert and looked up. "Was it true?"

I managed enough concentration to process back to what she was most likely referring to. Though I located it in an instant, an unexpected trouble blocked my vocal passages. It took some effort to continue on my candid way. "Yes." I set my eyes into hers. "I was lonely." I looked away. "Of course I was."

"Oh ... I'm ..."

"... Sorry you asked."

We made small talk in the dying seconds of lunch.

Striding from the clinic, the dressing hidden under my shirt so nobody could see what I'd been through, I felt only a slight chafe but didn't feel especially well. There was jelly at my centre: something loosened and shifting in a tender place. I put it down to shock—having so abruptly required the ruthless skill of a grave professional. Too, there was a benign guilt; after all, I'd just undergone a cancer operation, had had no pain, and walked now in the confidence of an excellent prognosis.

I feared that people could see it in my face.

LIZA'S GIG

One day Paul needed my van to help Bill move. I knew it wasn't such a good idea.

"Make sure you behave." I proffered the keys but held onto them.

"What are you talking about?"

"You know."

"We're not crazy."

"Yes you are."

"Okay. But Bill needs the help."

"I need that thing later on for Liza's gig."

"I know."

I tossed the keys and Paul snagged them with a steady quickness of hand. I felt better.

When I told Liza the van was gone and the reason why, she frowned. "It's the only vehicle we've got."

"I know. Try to think about something else."

"It's Saturday."

"It's still morning."

"It'll be afternoon soon. Then evening. We need to load up by six."

"I know."

She turned back to the keyboard. I stood in the doorway of her music room, magazine in hand. She began to play. I moved to the couch.

An hour later I surfaced from a dream. Liza was still singing. I rose and went to the kitchen, flipped on the kitchen radio and went for tuna, an onion, the can opener, mayonnaise, bread, the toaster, a knife, the kettle, water, the teapot. I began to chop the onion. Throughout this process I monitored talk radio. The news came on. Labour troubles, political doings, economic forecasts. Then the traffic person with a report from an airplane:

> ... Things are fine on most of the major routes with a slight slowdown northbound for all you Saturday shoppers trying to get across the Oak Street Bridge. Further uptown, there is a police incident involving an overturned van at Cambie and Sixteenth. Emergency vehicles are on the scene. Be sure and avoid that area ...

I dropped the knife, aware of the TV cliché my image would have evinced had I been videoed. The piano stopped. The radio talked on in voices assaultive. I jabbed the thing silent.

Liza was at the doorway. "What happened?"

"There's an overturned van near the bar."

"What do you want to do?"

I picked up the knife.

Liza shifted to lean against the jamb. "Maybe there's somebody we can call."

I put the knife back down. "Get the toast. I'll go on the bike."

"Okay."

"I'll be back in time for the gig."

"Don't worry about it."

In four minutes I was wheeling away up Hemlock, regretting the

Liza's Gig

fast start, puffing my lungs raw by the top of the hill, then turned at the base of Shaughnessy, flew down Sixteenth, made all the lights, and arrived in less than ten minutes. The scene was cluttered with motorcycles, fire fighters, one ambulance. I watched from the sidewalk. It had been a side-impact. A five-ton rental truck hammered them good from a trajectory down the slight hill of Cambie. Firefighters buzzed away with their nasty-looking power callipers, peeling away car metal. It had been a good van, old but well-maintained, a couple of years newer than mine.

Since I was in the neighbourhood I pedalled by the bar. They'd got the last parking spot. Bill's furniture was stacked inside. I didn't feel like a drink so I just stood for awhile and let raindrops tap my helmet. I wanted lunch.

For some reason I felt the need to open the door quietly and sneak the bike up the stairs. Liza was at the keyboard, her back to me, working in silence with headphones. I stooped close and wrapped my arms about her shoulders. Her exercised tendons warmed my hands through her thin blouse. She snuggled her neck to mine and sighed. Soon she would be on stage.

ARCH SOTS AND TOSSPOTS

Liza needed an event to network with some music types. I volunteered a dinner party. In an effort to avoid a disaster like last time I plotted to do it all myself, with no help from Paul.

"But I can come through this time." He stood in my kitchen, beer can poised to pour. "I'm nowhere near as fragile."

"Like hell. I'm never going through anything like that again."

"It wasn't so bad, was it?"

"How do you know? You weren't here for most of it. You were drunk as Dean Martin and mean as Josef Stalin."

"They say that's a myth about Dean Martin ..."

"Don't change the subject ..."

But even through the humour I could see Paul was hurt. It was during one of his new-prescription periods, when his mental state improved either by dint of the medication or, more probably, the mental effect of trying something fresh; of potential, of some hope of being better. His drinking was the same, of course.

Anyway, I opted for roast chicken, with a simple but impressive bocconcini salad; my own variation, with sweet onions, vine-ripened tomatoes, whole fresh basil leaves, and—my secret weapon—a raspberry jam vinaigrette. I toyed with the idea of some kind of soup: I am renowned for my French onion; have even been known to make a mean garbanzo purée. Ultimately I decided it would be too much labour, what with my plan to do two kinds of pie for dessert.

When Paul heard the menu he asked who all was coming.

"Oh, Simon and potentially someone with him. And these friends of Liza's from the music scene."

"Girls?"

"Yeah, I think so."

"What're their names?"

"What does it matter? It's a Thursday night. You'll be going to sleep about the time we sit down."

"I could book off." He took a seat at my cutting board. "Special occasion. The chance to meet new girls. You know."

I rolled pastry. "Yeah, well ..."

"Aw, forget it."

"I will."

"It's probably for the best. Friday's the richest day of the week." He drank. "And I'm broke as a twig."

I stepped to the fridge, crouching at the vegetable crisper. "How many lemons should I use?" I grabbed two.

He peered at the fruit in my hand. "I don't know. They look pretty hefty."

"The recipe says one but I like pie as lemony as hell. Lemony so that it smells like a citrus grove in my dining room. Acrid-lemony. Lemony so that you get tears in your eyes."

"You're not supposed to kill with lemon meringue pie, you know. You're not supposed to knock people on their asses."

"Why not?"

Paul took a lemon from my hand. "They are pretty big."

"I'm gonna take a chance with two."

"You're pushing it, the chemistry might go wonky on you. Baking's not like cooking, you know. The cornstarch might not react."

"Jeesh. I wouldn't want my cornstarch to not react!"

"Laugh if you want but it's a sad sight to see. You end up pouring the pie out like cold stew. The moisture will make the crust go like wet newspaper. Your meringue will drift with the breeze on top like an errant iceberg. I've seen it happen. Absolutely disgusting."

"I'd rather not add such a calamity to my repertoire of experience."

"Then you'd better reconsider." He gestured with his beer glass to my ragged-topped box of cornstarch. "Figure how much acid that stuff—as old as it appears to be—can take. Your thickening agent factor is critical. You should always be working with contemporary ingredients, by the way. The rule is, if it's older than the current federal administration, then throw it out."

"Thank you for that, Chef Paul. I guess pies toward the ends of the Trudeau and Chrétien governments were getting pretty dicey."

"And don't forget the zest." Paul often ignored my humour. "You gotta zest."

I wielded my cheese grater. "I am prepared to zest."

"Attaboy. See how urbane I am?"

"Yup."

"Really."

"Sure, I know you're urbane. You're urbane as all heck."

"So why don't I get an invite to these things?"

"Oh for cryin' out loud. You blew your chance last time."

"Hey a real friend would forgive. A real friend would be a real friend ..."

"Oh all right if you're going to get all depreciatory on me, attend already. Attend, by all means. I'm doing all the cooking anyway. We sit down at eight. But don't blame me if you're bored. I mean, I don't

Arch Sots and Tosspots

even know these people. They might be utter louts."

"A music crowd? Who knows. Louts and perhaps boors."

"Or worse."

"Sots, maybe."

"Sots and tosspots."

"Nothing worse than a table fulla souses and arch sots."

"In Shakespeare's time or in ours. He knew enough to call them out of the crowd."

"It's all there in the text."

"Are you sure you want to come?"

"Is Jeannie invited?"

"Are you kidding? And take a chance on whatever Mr Creepy she brings along damping down the whole soirée? Talk about your Elizabethan villains, your rapscallions and cutthroats, your general ne'er-do-wells. No siree."

"She's always interesting to talk to ..."

I gave Paul a look. He gave it right back.

"Forget about it. I don't care how long you stand there glowering." I looked down to the work at hand, chopping carrots, concentrating on not cutting myself and raising my voice above the noise. "I don't want any scenes. I don't want any delinquents going through my stuff. I don't want wine exploding inside my refrigerator."

"It wasn't that bad."

"You weren't there!"

That stopped him.

"Aw never mind. I'll be sleeping, anyway." He took another drink.

When Liza got home from work her mood wasn't as bright as usual.

She didn't have to say anything. I could tell by the curt note of her door-closing, the grim notes of her shoes upon the stairs.

"Sweetie!" I grabbed her before her coat was fully off. "You sexy thang, you. How was your day?"

"Tough. I'm so tired I could melt. What are we doing tonight?"

"Surely you jest, my love. We are entertaining. Your music world contacts. Various extras, perhaps. Dinner. Conversation. Who knows?"

"Oh god."

I sent her to bed.

Thankfully the first guest to arrive was Simon. Liza was still snoozing.

"Man, are you a sight for bleeding eyes. I hope you're not stoned into mental oblivion tonight."

"No, no ..." He held his arms wide open, a brown-bagged bottle in one hand. "What you see is what you'll never forget."

"Oh man. Great to hear."

"Who all is coming?"

"A bunch of Liza's music buddies. I think some of them might be downright young."

"Great."

"We'll find out, I'm sure." I took a mock glance past him. "No date, I see."

"Yeah, Joan and I are taking a break. There's somebody at the clinic who's up-and-coming but I didn't feel ready to expose her to one of these mysterio-comic freakouts of yours. Not just yet anyway."

"I'm glad you have things in perfect perspective."

"That's what you keep me around for."

"Right you are." I gestured with my vegetable knife toward the wine glasses. "Drink?"

"Not right now. I'll just slip out to the back for a sec."

While Simon smoked up I put the finishing touches to the salad and cut rounds of baguette for the cheese plate. The doorbell rang. I ran down and opened the door to trio of black-clad twenty-something women. They appeared surprised. An awkward pause let me fully see the depth of their misgivings and what appeared to be at least a mild disdain for what stood before them. I fought a compulsion to both gawk at them for their funereal dress—one had white body paint and a safety pin stuck in her face—and quip about it being too early for Halloween.

"Um. We're looking for Liza's place?"

I swung the door full open and stepped aside. "Ladies, you've found it!"

Our single-file troupe up the stairs was silence of the non-comfortable variety. At the landing I smiled as wide as possible. "Can I take your coats?"

"Um. I'll keep mine."

"Me too."

"Can I just lay my cape over the banister?"

"Of course. Liza is just rising from a nap right now, at least I hope she is."

"So you're, um ... Liza's boyfriend?"

"Yup."

"I'm Krysta."

"Winifred."

"Destiny."

We shook hands like business associates.

Liza popped out of the bedroom door. "Oooh, you guys are here." The ladies all traded hugs.

Simon appeared. "Whoa. Was there a dress code for tonight?"

"Hah ha. Say hello to Liza's music buddies. Krysta, Destiny, and ... Winnie?"

"Winifred."

"Got it. Simon, here, is a psychologist. So if you're feeling the least bit unstable, feel free to ..."

"... Keep it to yourself." Simon had found a glass and was pouring wine. "And drink with quiet desperation."

The women accepted this with somber countenance.

"Hah ha. He doesn't like to work off the clock. Not to mention stoned. But seriously, he'll speak with penetrating insight when called upon. That's what I keep him around for."

"Hah ha ..."

No one but me was laughing.

Simon kept his grin. "More interesting is the Holocaust resonance you guys elicit."

"Huh?"

"The 'I am dead' proclamation that especially ... is it Destiny?"

"Uh-huh."

"Especially Destiny's white-on-black visual iconography. There's no denying the elegance of casket regalia, the final fatal self-admission that the grave is only a matter of indeterminate time."

The girls stood silent and staring.

"I'm sure it's quite liberating." Simon continued his polemic. "There is equivalence in many cultures for a ritualized and sometime jovial celebratory kind of embracing of fate ..."

"Well, I can see this is going to be an interesting conversational extravaganza. Shall we proceed to more comfortable surroundings?" I managed to coax the assemblage from the hallway to seats in the living room. To my relief everyone present agreed to drink. This was a mixed benefit; things would inevitably loosen, something I prayed would happen sooner than later, but none of Liza's ghoulish gaggle had brought wine, beer, a flask, a cauldron or anything else resembling the traditional polite liquid contribution to a dinner party. I rued that my vino supply would be run over this night and left as dead as these girls seemed to be trying to look.

I put on some John Cage—the only "out there" music I owned—then dashed to refuge in the kitchen to get everything ready. I pulled a couple more bottles of white out of the cupboard and got them cooling in the fridge, then started in on drinking seriously myself.

The phone rang. A weird feeling that it might be important, and the fact it was so near at hand, made me violate my firm anti pick-up principle and get it. It was Paul. "I left my cigarettes."

"Huh ..." I looked around. "I don't see them."

"They're there. They've got to be there."

I walked with the phone into the living room. The pack was on an end table. I held a hand to the mouth-piece and grabbed them. The silent room stared at me.

I galloped back to the kitchen. "Yeah they're here. There's only three left. Why aren't you sleeping?"

"I was bugged, trying to remember where they were."

"Well now you know. Go to sleep."

"I actually was ... Did. I had a nightmare."

"Oh?"

"Yeah."

"So you called to tell me about it. In the middle of my dinner party."

"I had to talk to somebody."

"Well ... Gee. Okay. Was it a bad one?"

"The ditch in Richmond. Me in the cab, hanging sideways."

"Oh. I wondered when that episode was going to rear its ugly ass again."

"I mean. I survived, right?"

"Of course you did, Paul. You're alive. This is not a dream."

"I started shivering, even under the covers. I woke up and was shivering and sweating at the same time."

"Well you know. Sounds like you might be ready."

"For what?"

"Therapy."

"Gaa ..."

"Breathe deep."

"Man. That's a cold beer in the face."

"Forget about the rising water?"

"Whew. I gotta breathe. Yeah. I might get to sleep now ... Thanks. Hoo man. Okay."

"Atta boy."

"I think I'm gonna be all right."

"Glad to be of help."

"Yeah. Speaking of which, how's it going?"

"The dinner?"

"Yeah."

"It's fine. There's a good mix ... You want to come over?"

"Naw naw. I'll be okay. But thanks, eh."

"Don't mention it.

"Don't drink too much."

"You're a little late with that advice."

"Sounds like you'll need to keep your wits about you."

"That's actually darn true, it's measuring up to be a tetchy crowd. I'm a little past it already, too."

"Try to control your mouth. You'll thank me ..."

Once the food was on the table things did improve. In fact, from my perspective there finally occurred in my dining room the kind of free-for-all verbal melee I'd fought hard down the years to facilitate. The synergistic giddiness translated into complete lack of inhibition as far as risky conversation was concerned. My recall features fragments, though there were several recurring themes. One of them, about past relationships, got me expounding wistfully on wasted love:

"I sure do regret her heartbreak. There was no need for that."

"How did it end?"

"Nothing traumatic. I just stopped calling her."

"That's cold. And rude, too. "

"Well she was heading for a greater fall and I was getting uncomfortable. There was something disconcerting, too. She started buying me expensive gifts."

"Like what?"

"Designer clothes. A space pen."

"What's that?"

"The kind that writes upside down, has a special gel grip. I found out later the damn thing cost nearly a hundred bucks."

"So that kind of stuff turned you off."

"Yeah. Gifts. Eeew."

In the mind-fog enfolding my brain I cannot remember how that particular strain of conversation was resolved, but soon we were talking about an actor friend of mine with a drinking problem:

"So I'm pulling him out of the car, he clearly wasn't going to be walking on his own, and when I'm grabbing him by the middle, this weird sensation of something coming out of him jolts me. I leapt back, thinking I'd dislodged a colostomy bag or something. And there is this shimmery, foil thing sticking out of him. For a second I think maybe he's been wearing some kind of bullet protection body armour or one of those paranoid tin-foil shields to protect against alien brain waves. It takes me a minute to realize he's grabbed the wine bag out of one of the half-empty cardboard kegs he'd been mauling back at the gala, and stuffed it in his shirt. There was still enough in there to keep him pissed until morning at least. Or enough to start again the next day. I mean I drink plenty myself as you can see, but I don't fully understand drunkenness at that level ..."

We moved on to politics for a bit but it just ended up with Simon and me dominating the conversation. Thankfully we got back onto relationships—particularly as regards sex—and it was his turn to hold boldly forth:

"Oh man, for a while there I was indiscriminately screwing just for comic relief ..."

"Eeew. When was that ever okay?" One of the Goths—I'd forgotten their names by then—drew back in disgust. "Remind me to be glad I missed that era in male-female relations."

"Oh c'mon now, there has to be equivalents in each generation."

"Not if we can help it. We don't see that kind of men."

"You mean my kind of men?" I just had to stick my head into the line of fire. "Men like me."

"However you want to have it."

Simon rescued me: "Oscar Wilde once said the best way to deal with temptation is to yield to it. My thesis, vis-à-vis guys going after girls, is that the interesting, resourceful men are the ones with the problems. The dull ones, the ones characterized as solid, great guys in fiction and in lore, are simply not presented with the opportunity to dramatize themselves."

"Whatever that means …"

"Sounds like lame rationalization to me."

"That's so cynical! And weak, too."

"Speaking of which …" Simon smiled at me. "Tell the cat story."

"The cat story?"

"The one that lived under your bed. When you lived downstairs."

"There's not much to that one, you pretty much tell it by asking for it to be told."

"Oh?" The one I suspected was Destiny, darkened and narrowed her gaze. "You had a cat living under your bed?"

"I didn't know it was there. It was just a weird time."

"Oh come on." Simon wasn't letting me go. "There was sex involved."

"Well yeah. But that was kind of a corollary to the thing."

"What on earth are you talking about?" Liza was on the edge of exasperation.

"I told you about it."

"No you didn't."

"He was romancing some girl at the time." Simon spoke into his glass. "There was a fascinating metaphorical quality to what happened."

I tilted my head at him. "Maybe you should tell it."

"With pleasure." Simon dabbed a napkin to his mouth. "I consider it to be the definitive sexual-political story. It involves equal measures of sexism, racism, arrogance, naked lust and emotional neglect."

"Not to mention, apparently, cruelty to animals." Destiny was right with the tale.

"I didn't do a thing to the poor kitty. It got scared and ran under my bed, that's all."

"And stayed for …?"

"A couple of days, I guess."

"At least two days, if I correctly recall your telling of it those several years ago." Simon beamed around the table. "Close your ears if you, like myself, consider our host one of the best guys you'll ever meet." He ignored the ironic jeers of the semi-drunk Goths sitting about him. "This is a dark shadow of the man, the guy we all love but prefer not to fully know."

"Well thanks, but I wouldn't go that far."

"Indeed it's true. You are a man who helps his friends, lends money or gives it away, always includes everybody, wishes the best for everyone, seldom speaks ill of the absent, cooks excellent meals to which we are frequently invited ..."

"Stop it."

"Generally the best guy around. But one day he brought home this office girl. And because I lived upstairs at the time I saw the predatory look in his face. Carnal, raw."

"What the hell are you talking about?"

"I saw you. When you pulled up in the car. From my study window. As you held the door open for her. Whatever her name was. What was her name?"

"Ah, something. I'm almost remembering." I was more than aware of how increasingly wanton this story would sound without my recalling the woman's name. "Just a minute, I'll get it ..."

"Never mind. Suffice to say she was a sexy little thing."

"Hah." Liza spat out her miffed disapproval. The sound of this unnerved me more than the prospect of having Simon recount the tale with all his threatened X-rated embellishment.

"And she had that certain something in her eyes, that expectation, that hope. I hesitate to offer the *je ne sais quoi* cliché, but there's no other way."

"I'm not getting you, here." Krysta's mauve-tinged eyes were quizzical. "It seemed to me that she seemed optimistic for something other than sheer sex."

"How could you tell?"

"By the way she eagerly held his hand. She was affectionate. In a real way. I could tell from where I was watching and I could see it clear when I met her. A few days later."

I slapped my hand on the table. "You never met her."

He turned to me. "You're forgetting the bagel shop."

"We never ..." It came back to me, a day we'd had to walk a little further for a parking spot. "Oh yeah. But only for a few minutes."

"The way she hung off you. Her look. Her smile. The tilt of her head. She was nuts about you."

I don't mind saying I was vexed. Simon seemed about to give away as much of my life as he knew or could make up. It occurred to me that he likely had had an extra dose of the strong weed he customarily added to the wine.

"Not only that, you yourself said that the sex was transcendental."

"Transcendental?"

"That was the word you used, yes."

"I've never described anything in my life as transcendental. I don't even completely know what it would mean in terms of sex, or anything else for that matter."

"Don't try to pretend there wasn't a lovely girlfriend involved with the cat incident."

"Why is it so important?"

"Because, as I recall, you assured her during intercourse that there was no living thing trapped beneath you. She was freaked at the idea, you told me."

"I must have been drunk."

"Drunk?" Liza had been listening with a bravely placid expression. "Well that explains it."

"Naw, you can't put all this down to the martini marathon I was on." I paused, hoping to alter the course of the conversation by interrupting its pace. "I was a major womanizer in those days. Everybody knows."

"Is that all you've got to say?"

"Uh. Is there more you'd like to know?"

"Have you truly examined it? Why specifically did you turn your charm beam on this woman?"

"It's like owning a gun. Once in a while you have to whip it out and see if it still shoots."

"Whoa!"

"So male!"

"Fascinating analogy. Duh!"

"It fits, though. And by the way how can you accuse a man of such lemon meringue pie eminence of being excessively masculine? Anyway. Every so often, no matter how level you might feel generally, no matter how settled and over it and in control of yourself, you so want to whip it out and ... Well, who among us still has a sex life?"

"Whoa!"

"You girls, of course. Simon?"

"Sporadic."

"As for me, since fifty went past it's declining, of course. But still once in a while it flares up and you connect with your life and times through the simple crazy physical abandon of *laissez-faire* sexual slam-dancing."

"Oh how politely you put it." Liza was on the edge of outrage.

"Thank you."

"You mean to say you had sex with this woman just to keep your plumbing clear?"

"No no no. Sex all by itself at my age is dull in the extreme. No no. The attraction is the process. The first phase being charm. So I whipped out my charm and shot her with it. To see if I could still hit the target."

"Ohmigod, I can barely stand all this macho-western movie violence jargon."

"Sorry, but it's better than your building trades metaphor. Please don't mention plumbing again, okay? At least not for an hour or so."

"As long as you don't mention guns."

"Oh gee is this conversation ever going downhill."

"I wanna know about the cat." This from Destiny. Everyone looked at her.

"Well. She snuck under my bed."

"How did you know it was a she?"

"I didn't. It could have been a male." I thought for a moment, recalling our final confrontation, the malice emanating from those ovaline eyes. "Now I think of it, I'm sure it was female."

"Why would you treat your cat this way?" Destiny's solemnity stopped the flow.

"Oh, it wasn't my cat. Actually, that's the best part of the story. You see, as Simon mentioned, I used to live in the basement of this building. It showed up at the window one summer morning as I was waking. There were two of them, actually. They started roaming around my place as if they owned it. I think a thunderstorm had scared them into trespassing, but they sure made themselves at home once they'd broke and entered."

"What colour was the cat?"

"Which one?"

"The one that stayed. I assume you didn't have two cats under there?"

"No, only one stayed. She was orange. With white stripes."

"She."

"Yeah, she."

"You mean the one that stayed?"

"Yeah."

"Because the one that didn't—I assume it got away somehow—it was likely a boy cat." Destiny's pronouncements had an edge. "I sense that."

"I suppose you could assume it was a male. It acted like it was in charge."

I waited for a protest from somewhere around the table. If there was one it was sufficiently under breath to be inaudible.

Simon turned to Destiny. "I'm glad you're helping me make him stick to specifics."

"Now what the heck do you mean by that?"

"Never mind. Just tell the story."

"I'll tell it for Destiny. You've already heard it. I'm sure anybody who's known me for more than a day has heard it."

"I might have heard it before but I've forgotten certain things." Liza had been listening intently. "And you change it every time you tell it. I mean, I never knew it was an orange cat."

"What difference does the colour make?"

"A woman cares about colour. A woman cares about a lot of things you might not think a woman cares about."

"Sheesh."

"Still."

"Yeah still." I washed down a swallow of cabernet. "Why am I always the one yakking away? Don't you girls have anything to tell us? You can't let us middle-aged burnouts commandeer the whole conversation."

"Um. I don't know …"

"You don't know?"

"No."

"You don't know what? Why you don't talk? Or you don't know any talk to talk?"

"Um, it's not something we do, like …"

"Aw c'mon now, you're kidding, right? You mean you never just sit around and yak to your friends?"

"We text."

"And tweet."

"You should see my Facebook page."

"I do all that stuff too …"

"Um, sorry to change the subject, but. I mean." Krysta held up her fork as if hailing a cab. "This pie is so awesomely yummy."

"You like my dessert?"

"It's so lemonesque. How did you do that? I tried to make this once and it turned all goopy."

"I had divine guidance. Though to be honest, I resisted the advice of my spiritual advisor and used way more lemon than the recipe called for. Maybe the altitude around here is just right, or my cornstarch was so old it overreacted. Or who knows."

"It's killer. I mean, I never tasted something so into the flavour, you know? It's like there's a can of lemon furniture polish spraying right into my mouth. Weird."

"You make my night, Krysta. You're welcome here anytime."

"That's generous. Bravo, my friend."

"Well. Finally something turned out against anticipated results."

"I'm still curious." Destiny seemed to have taken no humour from the cat story. "What do you think is the source of your dysfunction?"

"The source? That sounds so social science. And dysfunction? Is it truly a fault you need to find here? Are we not talking of a simple human primal constituent? I mean, a house cat doesn't need claws but sharpens them every scratching post chance they get ..."

"Oh, cliché! You boomer boys are always falling back on some kind of organic empiricism to explain away your moral failings."

"Boomer boys?"

"Your whole privileged generation."

"Dems fightin' woids, lady."

"Ooh I'm so scared. Didn't you say your 'nature' is going down? Doesn't that include your general physical prowess? Aren't you afraid I'll pound the living crap out of you with this empty wine bottle?"

"I'll ignore your profligate insults if you pour me some of that other stuff by your elbow."

"That's another thing. Why is your cohort such a bunch of hopeless alkies?"

"Doesn't every human wave have its preferred intoxicant?"

"Maybe. But you guys are so grody."

"In short, you want me to explain myself."

"For goodness sake stop framing it and tell already. Though a full explanation would be pushing it, in view of how many times you've drained your wine glass." Liza was polite but firm. "But you're always entertaining, even drunk. So just make a stab at it. Take it in easy to swallow bites. Give us at least a semi-concise précis."

"Well I was born in a log cabin on the shores of Georgia Straight."

"Don't be silly."

"You wanted me to tell it, I'm telling it. I have to lay down the context, give you the full textual scenario."

"Did you deliver papers as a kid?" Krysta was getting into the spirit of kidding around. It made me smile.

"As a matter of fact I did! And that reminds me. Here's a good entrée to the story of my socio-political coming of age. Me and my friend Randy once got a tour through a 1963 Lincoln Continental."

"Whoa."

"And the thing that sticks with me about it, the thing that weirds me out is, my little friend and I were getting shown this brand new black land yacht. With the suicide doors that look like coffin lids and the open, vulnerable convertible top. Something you never saw in a place like Qualicum Beach. And within weeks maybe, that same year, anyway, JFK gets assassinated. Riding in a car just like this."

"Wild."

"Even at ten years old, I knew it was."

"That is an odd connection to history."

"And surreal. Standing as we were in the parking lot of the Snow White Motel."

"What was it called?"

"Snow White. This was before you'd get sued by Disney. It's not there anymore. It had cabins named after the Seven Dwarfs. I think it was Bashful, these folks were staying in. Friendly Californians, they were. I knew them from selling newspapers. They came up every year. Stayed in either Bashful or Doc …

"But anyway. This, believe it or not, leads onto what I'm trying to say. Our whole historical moment. Huge, wasteful cars. Political assassination. Americans. Angry conservatism. And the resultant imminent suffering of the period."

"Suffering? You guys suffered?" Destiny looked around. "That's really, um, far from what I would think."

"Not all of us. A chosen terrible sample. A million or so Asians and about sixty thousand of our American cousins."

"Oh. You mean Vietnam."

"Imagine if you will a complicated jungle conflict rising from a civil war in a place nobody ever heard of and a bunch of World War II generals who think they can waltz in there and conquer the situation with plain ol' American machinery and know-how and enemy body-counts in the thousands-per-battle. These clowns thought five-hundred-dead-per-week US casualties was no big deal. They create this awful Moloch—literally a young-man-eating machine—that became such an über-monster, such a mental-physical-emotional-social object of utter hatred and polarization that it caused a political schism in the collective world consciousness such that our hair and our music and our attitudes became picayune concerns in the overall miasma. And out of this massive disillusion our grand tradition of 'live for today', 'share the land', and 'question authority'—that last one's my favourite—became the creed of a whole statistical goliath, unstoppable and still being felt all over the world."

I took a drink, not liking how my impassioned monologue had silenced the room. "At least it was fun while it lasted."

"How do you mean?"

"Well, the live-for-today edict morphed into a live-for-yourself mandate. You can see that in the number of SUVs my boomer mates drive instead of walking to the corner store. The share-the-land idea fell apart when the smarter hippies surreptitiously bought their communal houses, kicked out their stoned roommates, and went to law school. They made some investments, took over city government, and converted their neighbourhoods into expensive boutiques. Et cetera." I waved my glass about to encompass the universe. "You can see how it all went."

"Is that all?"

"Isn't that enough?"

"What about all the privilege you guys have?"

"Privilege? Aw man. Heh. Boy, have I got an answer for that. First of all. And most important you have to understand. Not all of us made it. Not by a helluva long way. Despite how the X and Y and Z and A, B, C, D, E, F, G generations whine about it. Sure, every generation has its cadre of losers. But mine is overlooked and that's just my point. There's plenty of us boomers didn't get the jobs. Didn't buy up the houses. Didn't clog up the university departments and management suites. Not all of us are queued up ordering somebody younger to make us a latte.

"Most of us languished in dead-end office jobs or doing mindless manual labour. Most have trouble getting our cars fixed and can't figure out what we're doing in life. A lot of us tried to make lifelong friends and saw them stomp away. Lots of us looked for love and if we found that it left us just like everything else. Many of us sat raving in mail sorting rooms, pulp mill chemical chambers, cheque-writing computer payroll sweat shops, or hanging off the sides of mansions with paint brushes in our hands. So many of us struggled with substances and madness.

"Most of us never got the attention of the world but sure as hell ended up in detox, lost and bewildered. Some of us strove to capture time and failed as we should have. I know a lot of guys like me who tried to find salvation inside a line-up of women. None of us found anything we could remember the next day.

"Most of us have nothing to show for decades of familial attempts. Our few children are hostile and disinterested. Our creativity melted into the pool of mass culture that rose along with us. It was hard to get your name in the paper other than for petty crime, like possession of marijuana or careless driving. Hell, we used to have the police after us for no good reason, before the reign of civil rights, before casual litigation. But then that was a problem, too.

"We so fear censure and social humiliation, we are cowed and walk hunched over, so weighed down are our simple social interactions with possible mine-field explosions, mystified before the courts of political correctitude. We're the first generation, whether it's true or not, to have to admit we can't get a hard-on. And pretend we're not embarrassed that there's a whole industry to produce drugs to help us out with that.

"We do gloat, though, that the good things—our anti-war-ness, eco-consciousness, multi-culturation, and especially the music—are still current and going fine.

"But drunkards? Whew, man, you are correct in your assessment. I saw the slackest minds of my generation urinate their brains against the wall! By the way, I'm allowed to use that line because I once poured Alan Ginsburg a glass of wine while standing in Warren Tallman's kitchen. Look it up. Sorry for the name-dropping. Anyway, I can't speak for the women, they seemed to hold it together a lot better than the men. It's no wonder we see the rise of the Cougar. Men their age are cancelled. Most of the guys I know got drunk around 1973 and have scarcely drawn a sober breath since. They stopped seeing, thinking, living. You can tell by their taste; the resurrection of Harley-Davison as a corporate entity? Frank Zappa album cover collages? Gortex over thready jeans and tank tops? Grey ponytails on near-bald fifty-five year-old men? Yuk.

"It's like something out of Oliver Sacks ... the guy who doctored these dozing patients into consciousness for a summer one year decades ago. They went to sleep at a certain age, were suspended, then woke up for a time. And they were oblivious, of course, to what had transpired. They had not matured, beyond where they were when they took sick. Alks are just like that, I swear ... They age barely a day past the minute they take a serious drink, and then it's curtains mentally.

"Paul once asked me, 'How do you slow down time?' Try quitting drinking, I told him. Sobriety slows down time to a virtual stop, pretty damn quick. It'll arrest time in its little tracks, it will. Dead. Stopped on a nickel. Slower and deader than life inside drunkenness ...

"Anyway, my generation. We wincingly tolerate one another's drinking and driving. We quarrel over five-dollar bills and let the C-notes flow down our gullets. We fear death at the same time life bores us stupid. We tried to make our mark in the world but it was just a scuff on the floor as we went down. The ones who made it—the first five years or so of the boom—they don't know any of this stuff and care even less than you guys do."

"Who says we don't care?"

"Yeah. We have to live in the world you leave us."

"Hey, who said anything about leaving? We're not goin' anywhere just yet, little girl."

"I wish you would, though. You and your sexist hardwired attitudes."

"Yeah yeah yeah. You have to understand what we are ..."

"Do you understand what you are?"

"Good question. What are we?"

"Do tell."

"I'll give it a go, but no guarantees ... We writhe ..." My head swiveled inside slightly. I regretted the volume of the wine as I knew I would. "We writhe ... to understand, you might say. We hold still in staring query—this is some bad poetry I wrote about it one time—at a world which has invented us. Because we don't know what we are. Happy cherubs at daily frolic? Wandering searchers of knowledge and peace?

"Gardener in love with every leaf? Or just a lone branch against leaden sky. Fading alarm on a stolen car. Lost parakeet yearning for a cage. Distant drone of summertime lawn mower. Crows winging nightward at flagging day. Death-in-the-family ringing midnight telephone. Unexpected kilo on a bathroom scale. Or perhaps just a loose-laced running shoe ..."

Simon shifted in his chair. "Don't forget Paul."

"Apropos of ...?"

"Nothing in particular ..."

"No, I won't forget Paul. He should be here, by the way. Dang, I wish I hadn't frozen him out tonight." I swilled what was left in the bottom of my glass. "Those spindly limbs, that deep-lined face and beer-bloated gut. Hanging around with boozers is fun maybe. Pathetically curious. Maybe even anthropologically interesting. But sooner or later you get stomped in a parking lot. You get carted off to detox. You get evicted from your grow house. You get ignored and become obscure. You may do badly at work and never get promoted. You might get cancer, whether you smoke or not. You forget you drink to forget you're drinking to forget. You might philosophize but not say anything. You might live long but never grow up. You don't understand your relatives. You can go into therapy and pour your guts out but then all you've got is a mess on the floor. You try to rescue your friends and fail. Your friends can't help you either. Drugs and sex and booze don't answer anything anymore if they ever did. You run out of money. You run out of time. All you can remember is unimportant and boring to others.

"Yeah, Paul ..." I took my last drink of the night, ignoring everyone. "Mystified Paul. Abandoned Paul. Paul, hanging sideways, unconscious, in a sunken taxi-cab."

DENNIS E. BOLEN is a novelist, editor, teacher, and journalist, first published in 1975 *(Canadian Fiction Magazine)*. He holds a BA in Creative Writing from the University of Victoria (1977) and an MFA (Writing) from the University of British Columbia (1989), and taught introductory Creative Writing at UBC from 1995 to 1997. He is author of six books of fiction, the most recent of which is the novel *Kaspoit!* (Anvil Press). He lives in Vancouver.